spring breakdown

Other books by Melody Carlson:

Carter House Girls Series

Mixed Bags (Book One)
Stealing Bradford (Book Two)
Homecoming Queen (Book Three)
Viva Vermont! (Book Four)
Lost in Las Vegas (Book Five)
New York Debut (Book Six)
Spring Breakdown (Book Seven)
Last Dance (Book Eight)

Books for Teens

The Secret Life of Samantha McGregor series
Diary of a Teenage Girl series
TrueColors series
Notes from a Spinning Planet series
Degrees series
Piercing Proverbs
By Design series

Women's Fiction

These Boots Weren't Made for Walking
On This Day
An Irish Christmas
The Christmas Bus
Crystal Lies
Finding Alice
Three Days

Grace Chapel Inn Series, *including*

Hidden History
Ready to Wed
Back Home Again

carter house girls

spring breakdown

melody carlson

ZONDERVAN®

ZONDERVAN

Spring Breakdown
Copyright © 2010 by Melody Carlson

This title is also available as a Zondervan ebook.
Visit www.zondervan.com/ebooks.

Requests for information should be addressed to:

Zondervan, 3900 *Sparks Dr. SE, Grand Rapids, Michigan* 49546

This edition: ISBN 978-0-310-74809-0

Library of Congress Cataloging-in-Publication Data

Carlson, Melody.
  Spring breakdown / Melody Carlson.
     p. cm. — (Carter House girls ; bk. 7)
     Summary: The wealthy fashion students in Mrs. Carter's boardinghouse spend a
  quiet spring break in Florida until the boys from Crescent Cove arrive and heiress
  Eliza goes missing.
     ISBN 978-0-310-71494-1 (softcover)
     [1. Boardinghouses — Fiction. 2. Interpersonal relations — Fiction. 3. Spring
  break — Fiction. 4. Kidnapping — Fiction. 5. Conduct of life — Fiction. 6. Christian
  life — Fiction. 7. Florida — Fiction.] I. Title.
  PZ7.C216637Bg 2010
  [Fic] — dc22   2009013983

Interior design: Christine Orejuela-Winkelman

Printed in the United States of America

14 15 16 17 18 19 20 /DCI/ 20 19 18 17 16 15 14 13 12 11 10 9 8 7 6 5 4 3 2 1

spring breakdown

1

spring breakdown

"I'm sorry, Mother, but I refuse to spend *my* spring break in some disgustingly dirty third world country." Eliza rolled her eyes dramatically for the benefit of her captive audience at the Carter House breakfast table. "It's just peachy that you and Dad don't mind being inoculated with all those toxic shots just so that you can use filthy outhouses, be devoured by mosquitoes, and sleep in rodent-infested tents, but count me out."

Casey giggled and DJ glanced around to see if Grandmother was anywhere nearby. DJ knew Grandmother didn't like for the girls to use their cell phones at the table. But exceptions were sometimes made when it was a parent—especially when it was a parent of wealth or influence, like the Wiltons.

Eliza's forehead creased as she listened to whatever was being said on the other end of the phone. "Thanks anyway, Mother, but I'm passing. Honestly, I'd rather stay right here in boring old Crescent Cove than go with you guys to the ends of the planet. *Y'all have fun now.*" Then she snapped her cell phone shut and used a foul word.

"Eliza Wilton!" exclaimed Grandmother as she entered the dining room. "That's no way for a well-bred Kentucky debutante to speak."

"I'm sorry, Mrs. Carter." Eliza looked slightly embarrassed. "I'm just so frustrated with my mother!"

"Well, please do control yourself." Grandmother frowned as she sat down in her regular place at the head of the table and put her napkin in her lap. "Good morning, ladies."

Like well-trained robots, or Stepford teens, they all chirped back "good morning." And then Rhiannon asked the blessing. This was a relatively new development, but something that Rhiannon had volunteered to do and, when both DJ and Taylor had backed her, Grandmother had agreed and later on even acted as if it had been her own idea in the first place.

After Rhiannon said "amen," she turned to Eliza. "So . . . where is it that your mom wants you to go for spring break anyway?"

"*Nepal*." The way Eliza said the name of the country sounded as if she was swearing again.

"I've heard Nepal is an interesting place." DJ refilled her coffee cup. "I'd love to go there someday."

Eliza made a face. "Great, I'll ask my parents if you can take my place."

"The mountains there are beautiful," Kriti said quietly.

"If I wanted to see mountains, I'd go to Switzerland," retorted Eliza.

"I think a trip to Nepal sounds like a fun adventure." Casey stabbed her fork into a piece of pineapple. "I'd be happy to go too."

"Maybe you and DJ should flip a coin." Eliza broke her toast in half. "To see which one of you can go."

"Well, DJ would need a passport," said Grandmother wryly. "And with only two weeks before spring break, I don't think it's very likely."

"Too bad." Eliza directed her sarcasm toward DJ. "It would've been fun to see you coming home covered in mosquito bites and suffering from some rare form of tropical dysentery and—"

"*Eliza?*" Grandmother's brows arched in warning.

"Sorry, Mrs. Carter." She made a sheepish smile. "I was just joking."

"Well then ... " said Grandmother. "As it turns out, I've already made plans for DJ and myself anyway."

DJ stopped with her spoonful of yogurt in midair. "Plans?"

"Yes. The general has graciously given me the use of his Palm Beach home during the week of spring break."

"Palm Beach, Florida?" asked Eliza with interest.

"Yes, of course."

Now DJ wasn't sure whether to be pleased or irritated. On one hand Palm Beach might be somewhat pleasant—sunshine and sand—but on the other hand, why hadn't Grandmother asked her *before* accepting the invitation for both of them?

Grandmother smiled at DJ. "Doesn't that sound lovely, dear?"

"I guess so."

"You *guess* so?"

"To be honest, you kind of took me by surprise, Grandmother."

"But isn't it a pleasant surprise?" Grandmother looked so hopeful that DJ forced herself just to smile and nod.

"Palm Beach sounds good to me." Taylor glanced out the window where it was raining again. "And I'm sure you won't miss this weather."

"My thinking precisely." Grandmother rubbed her wrist. "My arthritis has been acting up lately, and I thought some warmth and sunshine would be most helpful."

"So ... " Eliza began slowly, directing this to DJ's grand-mother. "If you and DJ are in Palm Beach, does that mean Carter House will be vacated by everyone else that week?"

"Yes, of course." Grandmother put a spoonful of sugar sub-stitute into her coffee and stirred. "I couldn't have you girls left here unsupervised."

"No, no ... of course not." Eliza looked slightly miffed now, like maybe she'd planned on spending spring break in "boring old Crescent Cove." Actually, DJ wouldn't be surprised, since Eliza had recently developed a crush on a new guy at school. She probably hoped that she and Lane Harris would be dating by spring break. Perhaps she even imagined inviting him over to Carter House while everyone else was gone — and maybe they'd throw some huge house party and get into all kinds of trouble. Really, it wouldn't surprise DJ a bit. It seemed that Eliza was steadily spinning out of control — like she thought someone was giving prizes for teenage girls with the most messed-up lives.

"So perhaps you'd like to rethink your decision about va-cationing with your parents now." Grandmother peered curi-ously at Eliza.

"No, thank you." Eliza firmly shook her head. "I'd rather just go home to Louisville."

"And stay there by yourself?" Grandmother looked concerned.

"The household staff would be there."

Grandmother nodded sympathetically. "Yes, I suppose so ... " Now she smiled as if an idea was occurring to her. "You know, Eliza, the general's Palm Beach house is quite roomy. Perhaps you'd like to join us for — "

"*Grandmother!*" DJ felt alarmed now. The last thing she wanted was to be stuck down in Florida with Eliza Wilton for a whole week. And, besides, didn't Grandmother know how many things could go wrong during spring break—especially with someone like Eliza along?

"What is it, dear?"

"Don't you think you should consult me first?" DJ asked. "I thought it was just you and me going to Palm Beach and now you're inviting Eliza too." The dining room got very quiet now and DJ could feel all eyes on her. "I mean, what if I decided to invite someone else to come without asking you first? How would you feel about that?"

"Well … I suppose that would be acceptable. It's a very large house after all."

DJ looked hopefully at her other friends now. "Like what if Taylor or Casey or Rhiannon wanted to come." Then feeling bad, she quickly added, "And Kriti too—what if they all wanted to come down to Palm Beach? Shouldn't they be included too?"

"Are you saying you want to invite *all* the Carter House girls to come with us to Palm Beach?" Grandmother looked slightly appalled and not exactly pleased. DJ thought she had her grandmother over a barrel with this idea. Surely she'd reconsider her invitation to Eliza now.

"Why not?" said DJ. "It seems only fair. I mean, we shouldn't exclude anyone, should we? That doesn't seem very *polite*, does it, Grandmother?"

"Well … no, I suppose it's not." Grandmother smiled stiffly and looked around the table. "All right then … let's make this official. I'd like to extend an invitation to any of you who'd like to join us in Palm Beach for spring break."

"Really?" Casey looked hopeful.

"Yes. Why not?" Grandmother's expression got serious now. "Of course, you'll need to obtain your parents' permission first.

11

And I'll expect you to cover your own travel expenses. And to contribute to the cost of food and entertainment while we're down there. But, DJ is right, it's only fair to invite everyone along."

"I think that sounds awesome," said Casey. "I just hope my parents will let me go."

"You could tell them that airfare to Florida will probably be cheaper than to California," DJ told her.

"Good point."

"Count me in too," said Taylor. "My mom's touring the Midwest all month, and I'm definitely not into seeing the great American bread belt."

"I don't know if I'll be able to go." Kriti looked uncertain, like maybe she wasn't sure that she was really wanted.

"Wouldn't Palm Beach be more fun than being stuck in the city?" DJ asked her. "I'd think your parents would be glad for you to have some fun, Kriti."

"That's right," added Casey. "You've been working so hard on keeping your grades up. You need a break."

"If it would help, maybe Grandmother can talk to your parents for you," suggested DJ.

"Of course, I'm happy to speak to them." Grandmother nodded as if this new plan was becoming more appealing. "And to anyone else's parents for that matter."

Suddenly it seemed that everyone was talking at once, excitedly planning for bikini shopping and flight booking and parental coaxing, before Grandmother interrupted to remind them that it was time to leave for school.

Then the girls hurried to gather their bags and coats, rushing outside and trying to avoid the rain as they ran toward the two cars. This morning Rhiannon and Kriti were riding with Eliza in her little white Porsche. The others went with DJ. But as DJ started her car, it occurred to her that Rhiannon had been unusually quiet at breakfast. In fact, she'd never said a word, one way or the other, about joining them in Palm Beach.

DJ turned to Taylor, who was sitting in the passenger seat. "Do you think something's wrong with Rhiannon?"

"She did seem pretty quiet," said Taylor.

"I wonder if she's worried about money." Even as she said this, DJ felt pretty sure that was the problem. "I mean, she might not be able to afford Palm Beach for spring break."

"Duh." This came from Casey in the backseat.

DJ turned around to look at Casey while backing the car out of the driveway. "Okay, I know that's probably got something to do with it. But maybe that's not all. Because, now that I think about it, Rhiannon was quiet last night too. Is she okay?"

"I'm not supposed to say anything." Casey imitated zipping her lips.

"It's not something about Bradford, is it?" DJ glanced at Taylor. "I mean, he seems totally devoted to her."

"No, it's not Bradford," retorted Casey in a slightly know-it-all tone.

"Is it her mom?" asked Taylor.

Now Casey didn't say a thing.

"It is, isn't it?" persisted Taylor.

Still Casey remained silent.

DJ snickered as she drove toward school. "You're a great one for keeping a secret, Casey. You've pretty much divulged it has to do with Rhiannon's mom. Why not just tell us what's up? At least that way we can be praying for her."

"We know her mom's out of rehab," continued Taylor. "But has she fallen off the wagon already?"

"Don't say you heard it from me."

"So that's it?" asked DJ. "Her mom's using again?"

"That's what Rhiannon thinks. She hasn't heard from her mom for more than a week now. And they had been in contact almost every day before that."

"Well, my rehab counselor said that it's pretty common for a person in recovery to go back to their drug of choice … at least once." Taylor sighed. "It kind of seals the deal."

"Huh?" DJ was confused.

"It's like that last painful reminder that you don't want to go back to your old ways." Taylor tipped down the visor mirror and touched up her lip gloss.

"But you haven't had a drink yet, have you, Taylor?" Casey asked.

"No way." Taylor firmly shook her head as she tossed the lip gloss back into her bag. "But that's probably because I'm actually scared to go back to that place. I'm afraid that if I drink again, even if it's just once … well, that it'll be all over with and that I'll never get sober again."

"I suppose that's a healthy fear," admitted DJ. "But you're a strong person, Taylor. I'll bet you'd get it back together—even if you did slip up."

"Maybe … but I just don't want to go there." Taylor was counting something on her fingers now. "Do you realize that I'm almost up to seventy-five days of sobriety now?"

"Congratulations!" DJ smiled at her. "We should throw you a party."

"No, thanks. I'll pass."

"Back to Rhiannon," said Casey. "What should we do?"

"I don't know what we *can* do." DJ pulled into the school parking lot, snagging a spot not too far from the main entrance. "I mean, besides praying and being understanding."

14

"I know something we can do," said Taylor as they got out of the car. "We can all help get some money together for Rhiannon to go to Palm Beach with us. That might help distract her from her mom's messes."

"Yeah, she could focus on our messes instead," teased Casey.

"Actually, that's a great idea," said DJ as they hurried across the street. "I'm willing to contribute whatever I can for her."

"I wish I could help too," said Casey. "But I'll be doing good if I can get my parents to agree to pay my way."

Just then Taylor pointed to where Eliza and the others were going into the building ahead of them. "Maybe we can get Ms. Eliza Wilton to pitch in for Rhiannon. We all know she can afford it."

"We know she *can* afford it," said DJ. "But the big question is will she willingly fork it over?"

Taylor chuckled like she knew a secret. "Oh, I think we might be able to come up with some ways to influence her."

"But what if Rhiannon won't accept charity?" asked Casey as they jogged up the steps to the door. "She can be pretty sensitive about that kind of thing."

"Somehow, we'll figure it out," DJ assured them. "Somehow, *all* of the Carter House girls are going to make it to Palm Beach for spring break." Of course, even as she said this, she had some serious doubts. Was it really a good idea for all of them to be down in Florida together? What if things got out of hand? Even worse, what if Taylor fell off the wagon? Suddenly DJ envisioned the Carter House girls starring in a bad episode of *Girls Gone Wild*, with her grandmother having a major meltdown, and everything just totally falling apart. But then she realized how ridiculous that image was and she couldn't help but laugh.

"What's so funny?" Casey shook the rain off of her jacket.

"I was just imagining spring break turning into spring breakdown." DJ chuckled.

"And what would be surprising about that?" asked Taylor.

As DJ hurried to first class, she had to wonder ... what *would* be so surprising about that?

2

spring breakdown

"I don't know why you even let it get to you, Rhiannon." DJ recognized Bradford's voice as she and Casey went up the stairs to the front porch, but his tone sounded sharper than usual.

"Hey," DJ called out in warning.

Bradford and Rhiannon both turned, making what seemed like forced smiles.

"Nice evening," said Casey as they walked past the couple standing in the shadows of the porch.

"You guys just getting back from soccer practice?" asked Rhiannon.

"Actually, it was a game." Even in the dim light, DJ could see that there were tears in Rhiannon's eyes.

"Yeah," added Casey. "We won."

"Good for you," Bradford said stiffly.

"Yeah . . . congrats . . ." Then Rhiannon turned away.

"See ya," called Casey as she and DJ hurried into the house.

"Wonder what's up with them?" DJ said after the front door was closed.

"Sounded like a lovers' quarrel to me." Casey slung down her bag at the foot of the stairs. "I'm going to run and see if there are any leftovers."

"Not me." DJ smirked. "I get to have *real* food tonight."

Casey looked disappointed. "Conner?"

"Yeah. You can come along if you like."

"Thanks, but no thanks. Being a third wheel isn't my idea of fun."

DJ hurried up the stairs. Conner would probably be there any minute, and she wanted to dry her hair before he arrived.

"Hey, Soccer Girl," called Taylor as DJ entered their room. "How'd the game end? It looked like you girls were kicking ... uh ... I mean you were totally creaming them before I left."

"That was pretty much the deal." DJ tossed her bag down and kicked off her shoes. "And thanks for coming. It's nice to have support."

Taylor chuckled. "Yeah, girls' soccer doesn't exactly draw in the big crowds, does it?"

"It might if you played." DJ pointed at Taylor, who was partially dressed and exposing a whole lot of skin.

Taylor laughed even louder. "Maybe that's the problem. You girls need to get skimpy uniforms like those professional volleyball girls wore in the Olympics. You'd probably really bring in the fans then."

"I don't think those are the kind of fans we're going for." DJ reached for the hairdryer and went to work. She was nearly finished when Rhiannon knocked on their door.

"Conner's here," she told DJ quietly.

"Big date?" asked Taylor with mild interest.

"We'll be eating some *big* food." DJ peered closely at Rhiannon now. "Are you okay?"

Rhiannon shrugged and glanced away.

"What's going on?" Taylor asked with genuine interest.

"Yeah," added DJ. "What's up?"

"My life." Rhiannon sank down onto DJ's bed now. "Or maybe it's down. I'm not even sure."

"Wanna talk?" asked DJ.

"But Conner's waiting for you."

DJ glanced at the clock by her bed. "Yeah, I should probably go. But it seems like you need to talk ... "

"Rhiannon can talk to me if she wants," offered Taylor.

DJ tossed Taylor a grateful look and then squeezed Rhiannon's shoulder. "That's a great idea. And then maybe we can talk some more when I get back, okay?"

Rhiannon nodded and almost seemed to be blinking back tears.

"There's really not much to talk about," Rhiannon said to Taylor as DJ grabbed her bag and hurriedly touched up her lip gloss. "You probably already heard about my mom."

As DJ was going out the door, she heard Taylor saying how she understood, "... probably more than you can even imagine."

Although she knew it was her own choice, DJ felt a tiny stab of envy, or maybe it was regret, at being left out. But DJ also knew that what Taylor had just said was true. Between Taylor's alcoholic dad and her own stint in rehab, she'd been through a lot. Also, she had changed a lot—not just in regard to drinking, but as a Christian too. Hopefully she'd have something helpful to say to Rhiannon. And instead of feeling jealous, DJ decided just to pray for both Rhiannon and Taylor.

"You seem pretty quiet tonight," Conner said after they'd ordered their food at the Hammerhead.

"Sorry." She pushed back a strand of loose hair and smiled.

"Anything wrong?"

She considered telling him about Rhiannon, but wasn't sure if Rhiannon would want her to. "Just friends, you know," she said as she stuck a straw into her soda.

"Friends?" His smile looked amused.

"Yeah . . . Rhiannon and Taylor were having a little conversation . . . I had to leave."

"A catfight?" he said in a way that sounded almost hopeful, like she was about to impart some juicy details.

"No." She shook her head.

"Sorry." He held up his hand defensively. "It's just that I remember a time, not too long ago, when Taylor and Rhiannon were sworn enemies."

"What?"

"You know, back when Taylor stole Bradford from her."

DJ waved her hand dismissively. "That was a long time ago."

"Like six months, maybe."

"Yes, but another lifetime." DJ looked evenly at him. "The truth is Taylor was being really nice to Rhiannon. They were talking about something important . . . and I had to leave."

"To be with me?" He looked slightly hurt now.

She forced a goofy grin. "Yes, to be with you. And just for the record, that's where I wanted to be." She nodded toward the kitchen. "Plus, there's food involved. Pretty much a win-win, if you ask me."

"That sounds more like my DJ."

DJ couldn't put her finger on exactly why it was, but something about that "my" word put her on edge. It wasn't like

20

Conner owned her. And she knew that wasn't what he really meant. Even so, it bugged her.

"I heard that you girls are heading down to Florida for spring break," Conner said after their food was delivered.

"How'd you hear that?"

"Harry told me."

"Wonder who told Harry?"

"One guess."

DJ considered this. "Well, a month ago, I would've said Eliza, but—"

"Bingo."

"Why would Eliza tell Harry about that?"

"Why do you think?" Conner had a sly look now.

"Do you think she's still trying to get him back?"

"Don't you?"

"Not really. I mean, she's been acting like Lane Harris is all that. I figured Harry was history. Plus, he's still flirting with Taylor like he thinks he's got a chance."

"Meaning he doesn't?"

"He might. But Taylor is trying to stick to her program … you know … and Harry is, well, not exactly predictable."

Conner's brow creased. "Yeah, I know. I thought he was really trying to give up his party boy ways and then just last weekend, he goes out and gets wasted."

"Really?"

Conner lowered his voice. "Well, he doesn't want everyone to know, particularly Taylor, but he was visiting Princeton, checking it out for next year since that's where everyone in his family usually goes. And he told me that he went to a frat party … and I'm sure you can imagine what happened."

"Maybe." She frowned. "But I'd rather not."

"I actually feel kind of sorry for poor Harry."

21

"Poor Harry?"

"Oh, you know, he means well . . . but he's kind of easily pulled in."

"Oh . . . "

"Speaking of college," he said suddenly, "Coach Davis told me that I might be getting scouted during our playoffs at spring break."

"Seriously?"

Conner nodded as he took a big bite of his fish.

"Very cool."

"Yeah." Conner chewed quickly. "Coach has a buddy at Wesleyan."

"Isn't that where your dad wants you to go?"

He nodded again.

"So your dad must be pretty jazzed."

"He is. And I guess I am too."

"So you've decided you want to go there for sure?"

He shrugged now. "It's not exactly Harvard or Yale, but it wouldn't be too bad. And they're definitely into soccer." He peered at her. "How about you?"

"Me?" She picked up a fry. "You mean as in Wesleyan for me too?"

"Why not?" He grinned. "Then we could be together."

"I suppose I could apply there, although it might be too late to get in next year. Grandmother actually made me send an application to Yale." DJ laughed loudly. "Like that's going to happen. But at least it made her happy."

"Yale?" Conner looked understandably confused.

"I know, it's a bit incongruous, but that's where her father went."

"Oh." He seemed surprised. "So are you into that whole Ivy League thing?"

22

"I don't really know." DJ sprinkled more vinegar on her fish and chips. She wasn't about to tell Conner that her friend Caleb Bennett was going to Yale next year and seemed quite happy about it. But then Caleb was twenty and he'd already done two years of junior college. He had firm goals and a much better idea of what he wanted to do with his life than she did. At this point DJ wasn't even sure she wanted to go to a big college, and Yale seemed like another world to her.

"Bradford is probably going to Yale," Conner told her as he squirted ketchup onto his fries. "He's got about ten generations who've gone there ahead of him, so it's pretty much a shoo-in."

"Rhiannon is applying to NYU as a backup, but she really hopes to get accepted to the Fashion Institute of Technology."

"Can you believe that in less than three months we'll all have graduated?"

DJ had to laugh. "I don't think we all seem old enough to be out on our own just yet."

"According to what Harry said about that party, a lot of college kids aren't old enough either." Conner looked concerned now. "So are you really going down to Florida too?" he asked. "With the rest of the Carter House girls?"

She picked up a fry. "Well, yeah. I mean, it was originally just going to be Grandmother and me and suddenly it was like everyone was going. Maybe not everyone — Kriti, Casey, and Rhiannon still aren't one hundred percent sure."

He shook his head in a dismal way. "I don't know, DJ . . . a bunch of you girls down there in Florida during spring break . . . Sounds like trouble to me."

She sat up straighter. "What's that supposed to mean?"

He shrugged. "You know."

"I know what?"

"Girls like Eliza and Taylor —"

"Taylor has changed," she shot back at him. "She's not a party maniac anymore. As for Eliza ... well, she could easily fall apart. But that's her problem."

"Unless she drags others with her."

"I don't expect Eliza to be dragging me anywhere with her." DJ could hear the edge in her voice now.

"Sorry." He suddenly looked truly contrite. "I didn't mean to suggest you would." Now he smiled. "I guess I'm just going to miss you, DJ. I'd hoped that you might be sticking around for spring break."

She softened. "The truth is I'd rather stick around town. But I doubt my grandmother would allow it. She plans to shut Carter House down for the week."

"What about your soccer?"

"Our finals are the week after spring break."

"Oh ... "

She reached over and put her hand on his. "I think it's sweet that you're going to miss me, Conner. That's kind of how I felt when you were gone during Christmas."

He pointed his finger at her. "But you went off to Vegas."

"Like that was so much fun, but thanks for reminding me." She rolled her eyes. "And besides, from what I've heard, Palm Beach is mostly inhabited by old rich people—not exactly the wild party crowd."

"Well, maybe things won't go nuts," he said. "Especially with Taylor still on the wagon."

"That's what I'm hoping."

"As long as she stays on the wagon."

DJ stifled the urge to defend her roommate. After all, time would tell. But so far DJ had no reason to question Taylor's resolve to remain clean and sober. Hopefully nothing, not even spring break in Florida, would change that.

"How's Rhiannon doing?" DJ asked Taylor when she entered the room that evening. "Did you guys have a good talk?"

Taylor looked up from her homework. "Pretty good . . . but she still seemed bummed."

"Do you think I should talk to her?" DJ tossed her bag onto a chair.

"I don't know. I mean, it might help . . . but it might be better just to give her some space too."

"Was it mostly about her mom?"

"Her mom, her life, her roommate—"

"Well, of course." Realization hit DJ. "Poor Rhiannon's been pretty much thrown to the lions."

"You mean the *lioness*." Taylor held up her hands like claws and hissed. Then she laughed. "And to think I used to have the B-word title around here."

"I wonder if Eliza isn't more of the problem than we know."

"She's definitely a *part* of the problem." Taylor nodded as she set her economics book aside. "But it's a lot of things. Even Bradford seems to be wearing on her these days."

"Bradford?"

"Yeah. He's acting like she's no fun, like she's too serious, and like he wants to have fun during his senior year."

"Fun?" DJ frowned. "Like what kind of fun?"

"What do you think?" Taylor laughed. "Harry comes back from Princeton telling his buddies about all the so-called fun he had on campus and suddenly poor little Bradford feels like he's missing out."

"I just don't get how some people define fun."

"Oh, I get it," Taylor said slowly. "I get it more than I'd like to remember. But I just don't want to go back there. The truth is it's not fun. Not really."

"I'm so glad you can see that now."

"But I'd be lying if I didn't say partying has a certain allure . . . or that I sometimes get tempted."

DJ sat down across from Taylor, studying her. "Okay, so tell me, what exactly is so tempting and alluring about getting stink-faced drunk?"

"It's not the stink-faced part, that's for sure. But there is something about that whole just letting go kind of thing. You know, forgetting that you have problems and just getting lost in the moment."

"But why can't you do that *without* alcohol?"

"Sometimes I can."

"How do you do it?"

"Through music or Pilates or a good book. There are ways. But I'm still a beginner, DJ. You're probably better at this kind of thing than I am."

DJ thought about it. "Yeah. I lose myself in things like sports or being with friends or good food. And sometimes dancing kind of takes me away."

"Dancing." Taylor stood up and acted like she was ready to get down. "That's actually a good idea. I'll have to put that on my list."

"And God," added DJ. "I'd have to put that at the top of my list."

Taylor nodded. "Yeah, me too."

"Anyway, back to Rhiannon. Did you tell her our idea about helping her to go to Florida?"

"Actually I did." Taylor sat back down.

"And?"

"And she turned me down. Flat. She made it crystal clear that she was not into charity. She said she'd rather spend spring break at her great-aunt's house than be a freeloader."

"Oh."

Taylor shrugged. "Seemed like there wasn't much more I could say."

DJ felt disappointed as she got out her laptop to finish her own homework. She'd really hoped that Rhiannon would come to Florida too. Partly for selfish reasons—because DJ knew that Rhiannon would help to keep the group balanced if things tried to get out of hand.

The next morning, DJ went out of her way to be especially nice to Rhiannon. "Wow, you look stunning," she told her as they went into the dining room for breakfast. "Is that an outfit you put together recently?"

Rhiannon looked down at her fringed suede jacket, short denim skirt, leggings, and retro cowboy boots and just shrugged. "Not especially."

"Well, it looks awesome." DJ nodded. "I wish you'd help me with my wardrobe."

"Are you feeling okay?" Rhiannon asked.

DJ shrugged. "Well, besides fashion challenged, yeah, I guess."

"Since when do you care about how you look?" jabbed Eliza.

DJ made a face as she sat down.

"But you are right," proclaimed Eliza. "Rhiannon has a very good sense of style, even if her style isn't for everyone."

"Thanks," muttered Rhiannon, "I think."

"No, I'm serious," continued Eliza. "In fact, I thought I might commission an outfit from you."

"Huh?" Rhiannon looked shocked.

"Are any of you going to the Rockabilly dance next week?" asked Eliza. "It's the Friday before spring break."

"Rockabilly?" DJ frowned. This didn't sound a bit like Eliza.

"Lane Harris told me about it," Eliza continued lightly. "It's a benefit dance for the March of Dimes. His mom is on the committee."

"Are you going?" asked DJ.

Eliza's brows arched. "Well, it's not official . . . yet. But Lane told me it was a Sadie Hawkins-style dance, which I take as a hint that he'd like me to ask him. So here's what I'm thinking—we should all go, to support the charity, of course. But we should all hire Rhiannon to help us with our outfits." She looked at Rhiannon. "I'm pretty sure you could swing a Rockabilly outfit with no problem."

"I actually like that look," Rhiannon said slightly defensively.

"And so do a lot of other people," DJ added, equally defensively.

"Me too," Taylor agreed. "In fact, I think those boots are wicked cool, Rhiannon. Can you help me find a pair too?

Not exactly like them, of course, but something retro and unique."

"Sure." Rhiannon brightened now. "It would actually be fun."

"So, are we all in?" asked Eliza hopefully. "Will you girls talk your guys into taking you to the Rockabilly dance?"

It was hard to tell whether or not there was total consensus. Not surprising, since Eliza was the one trying to get this ball rolling. But after some coaxing (from Eliza) Kriti halfheartedly agreed, and Taylor said she thought it sounded like fun. Casey, however, wasn't showing much enthusiasm. So DJ decided, for Rhiannon's sake, that she'd encourage Casey to get on board as well. DJ hoped that Casey would invite someone besides Garrison and, since they'd been sort of on-again-off-again, it seemed likely. Anyway, DJ felt hopeful for Rhiannon's sake. With everyone needing wardrobe help, Rhiannon might be able to make enough money for her airfare to Palm Beach, and maybe she'd accept some friendly donations after that. Plus, working on clothes for her friends would keep her distracted from obsessing over her mom.

By the end of the day, it seemed that everyone was agreed. All six Carter House girls, plus their guy friends, would be attending the Rockabilly charity dance. And Rhiannon was in charge of their outfits. So far, so good. Although, as they sat around the dinner table, DJ got the distinct impression this was not going to be smooth sailing.

"Lane seemed quite pleased that I asked him to the dance," Eliza announced. "And just as pleased that I'd encouraged you all to come as well." She smiled happily at the group. "And just so you know that I'm actually a very benevolent person, I have offered to purchase all of our tickets."

Naturally, they all thanked her, and Grandmother commented on how generous this was of Eliza. "So, we know Eliza is going to the dance with Lane," continued Grandmother. "Which is simply wonderful since Lane's family are old friends of mine." She beamed at Eliza. "I actually think your parents will be quite pleased to hear that you're friends with that boy. But how about the rest of you? DJ, I assume you'll be going with Conner?"

DJ nodded as she chewed her food.

"And Rhiannon with Bradford?" said Grandmother.

"That's right," Rhiannon supplied. "And he's letting me put together his outfit too."

"How about you, Taylor?"

Taylor cleared her throat and sat up straighter. "I invited Harry Green."

Eliza stiffened, her eyes narrowing. "Big surprise there."

"I told him it's just as friends." Taylor didn't even look at Eliza. "And that it's for a good cause."

"Very nice," said Grandmother. "How about Casey and Kriti? Who did you girls invite?"

Kriti looked embarrassed. "Josh Trundle," she said quietly.

"Nice boy." Grandmother nodded. "Casey?"

"Seth Keller," Casey muttered.

Both DJ and Taylor looked at Casey in surprise. Seth had most recently been Taylor's boyfriend. Even after she'd broken up with him, he hadn't given up on her.

"And he agreed to go with you?" asked Taylor.

"It's not like I put a gun to his head," Casey shot back.

"No, I didn't mean —"

"You guys broke up a long time ago," continued Casey.

"That's not what I'm saying," Taylor tried. "I just meant that —"

"You're certainly not the one to talk about stealing boy-friends," sniped Eliza.

"I wasn't talking about—"

"Let's see," continued Eliza. "First you stole Bradford, and then Seth, and you even flirted with Conner once, and now it's Harry, and—"

"I don't see how I can steal something that doesn't—"

"Girls! Girls!" Grandmother clapped her hands sharply. "That's enough!"

"Isn't the purpose to go and have a good time?" DJ asked hopefully.

"And to raise money for a good cause," Kriti quietly added.

"Absolutely." Grandmother nodded. "And to act like ladies."

"I think getting the clothes together is going to be so fun," Rhiannon said with enthusiasm. "I already have a few cool pieces, but I'll do some shopping this weekend and hopefully I'll have some things ready for you guys to try on by the middle of next week."

"I plan to do some shopping this weekend too," Eliza announced.

"Big surprise there," Taylor said wryly. "Isn't shopping your favorite hobby?"

"I am quite good at it." Eliza tipped her nose in the air. "But I plan to head into the city to pick up some things for Palm Beach. Anyone who wants to join me better speak up since you know my car's not very big."

"You're going to the city?" Rhiannon said hopefully.

Eliza looked pleased. "Want to come along?"

"Well, there are a lot more retro shops there and—"

"No, I meant for *real* shopping, Rhiannon—for Palm Beach."

"If you want a cool Rockabilly outfit, you might want to consider what I'm doing as *real* shopping too. But if you don't want to give me a ride, I can—"

"No, no, it's okay. And maybe we can kill two birds with one stone. I'll let you do your rag-bag shopping and then you can come with me to some of the more elite shops. Who knows? I might even pay you in advance for putting together my dance outfit."

Rhiannon's eyes brightened.

"Anyone else?" asked Eliza hopefully. But there were no takers. And, although DJ was relieved that Eliza was getting excited about gathering some outfits for the rest of them, she had no intention of going along. Besides, she and Casey had a soccer match on Saturday morning. Thankfully, they would be busy.

"I have some wonderful news," Grandmother announced at breakfast on Friday. "I know all you girls will be absolutely thrilled to hear it." The table got quiet now and Grandmother continued. "I contacted a designer friend of mine yesterday." She looked coyly around the table now. "I know you've all heard of Juicy Couture." She waited for their reaction, which on the most part was high interest.

"You have connections with Juicy Couture?" Even Eliza seemed impressed.

Grandmother waved her hand. "You have no idea what kind of connections I have." She chuckled. "And the things I hear in regard to the fashion world."

"What's up with Juicy?" asked Taylor.

"Well, you may have heard that designer Josie Feldman left Couture last year, but the latest news is that she's now developing her own line of swimwear."

"That's your *wonderful* news?" DJ looked blankly at her grandmother. "That a designer is making swimwear?" Talk about a letdown.

Grandmother scowled. "That's not all, Desiree."

DJ tossed her grandmother a warning look.

"Excuse me, I meant to say DJ." Grandmother looked slightly apologetic.

"I've heard of Josie Feldman," said Rhiannon eagerly. "She's an excellent designer."

"Precisely. And now she's paid her dues and is developing her own line. It's simply called Josie, and it will be more affordable and quite possibly more popular than Juicy Couture."

"That doesn't seem likely." Eliza looked unimpressed. "Most cheaper spin-off lines usually don't last very long in the marketplace."

"Tell that to Vera Wang or Isaac Mizrahi," Rhiannon shot back.

"Touché," said Grandmother proudly. "Our little Rhiannon pays attention to the trends—something any designer worth her salt should do."

"Yes, Grandmother." DJ was eager to escape this conversation. "But what does any of this have to do with us?"

"Josie Feldman wants to use you girls as models for her new swimsuit line." Grandmother waited expectantly for their reaction, which seemed to vary between enthusiasm and curiosity, and for DJ just plain confusion.

"When are we going to be doing this?" asked Eliza with mild interest.

"It seems a little late in the season to be selling a new swimwear line," added Rhiannon.

"Yes, it is rather late. But Josie plans to offer her swimwear online for the first season. Her hope is to create a buzz among customers, and she's got a certain celebrity lined up—I can't release the name just yet, but trust me, this girl is quite popular. Anyway, with the celeb endorsement and some success, Josie will put together a more complete catalog next winter and hopefully get some accounts set up with some of the mid-priced department stores. Then she's off to the races."

"I still don't get it," said DJ. "What are we actually supposed to do?"

"A photo shoot, obviously." Grandmother's voice was laced with impatience. "And Josie was delighted to hear that we had plans to go to Palm Beach during spring break."

"She's going to shoot us down there?" asked Taylor.

"Exactly. But not only that." Grandmother clapped her hands with glee. "Josie has offered to cover our travel expenses plus a little extra in exchange for your cooperation in the shoot. Therefore our Palm Beach trip will cost us next to nothing."

Now the reaction to this bit of news brought even more enthusiasm. Not necessarily from Eliza, since money was inconsequential to her. But Rhiannon's eyes lit up like she was truly excited at the prospect of a free vacation. And this was enough to pull DJ fully on board as well. She'd been worried that, despite Rhiannon being able to make some money on their dance outfits, she still wouldn't have enough for Palm Beach. And DJ really felt Rhiannon needed to go. So, even if it did mean DJ had to pose in front of a camera, which she loathed, she was willing. After all, didn't the Bible say that a friend was willing to lay down her life for a friend? And if biting the bullet for fashion wasn't friendship, what was? She just hoped bikinis wouldn't be involved.

4

spring breakdown

"You girls are doing a *swimsuit shoot* in Florida?" Lane said this loudly enough that it seemed the whole cafeteria stopped to look and listen.

Eliza looked slightly embarrassed now, acting like she was trying to hush him by placing her forefinger over her lips.

"A swimsuit shoot?" echoed Harry from the other end of the table. "Who for? *Sports Illustrated*?"

DJ laughed so loudly she snorted. "Yeah, right."

Conner looked at her with curiosity. "What's going on anyway?"

"Don't tell me the Carter House girls are going to do a calendar?" Seth let out a low whistle. "Count me in."

"No, silly." Eliza firmly shook her head. "It's for a new designer."

"Seriously?" Harry peered hopefully at Taylor. "When is this shoot taking place and are you selling tickets?"

"Very funny." Taylor rolled her eyes as she picked up her fork.

"The shoot will be in Palm Beach and—"

"Palm Beach?" Lane said suddenly. "Palm Beach, Florida?"

"Duh." Casey shook her head like she was questioning his mental capacity. "You already knew we were going to Florida."

"But my grandparents have a house in Palm Beach!" Lane declared this like it was vital information. "Right on the beach!"

"So?" Taylor just shrugged. "I'm sure a lot of grandparents have homes down there since ninety percent of the population is probably old people."

"So? I'll bet I could use their house during spring break," he continued with excitement. "Gram and Gramps are —"

"Gram and Gramps," parroted Eliza. "That's so sweet, Lane."

"Thanks, but my point is they're off on some month-long cruise — and their house is just sitting there vacant."

"Hey." Harry grinned at Lane. "My man! How about inviting a few good friends to join you for a week at the beach?"

The next thing, it seemed that all the guys — all the guys except Conner anyway — were making plans to join Lane at his grandparents' beach house in Palm Beach for spring break.

"That's crazy," DJ told Lane. "No grandparents in their right minds would let a bunch of teen boys use their home during spring break."

"You don't know Gram and Gramps." Lane winked at her. "I'm their favorite."

"Still . . ." She just shook her head.

"This will be totally awesome," Eliza chirped happily. "A week-long beach party with the guys along too!"

"Totally awesome," DJ repeated with sarcasm. "I can so hardly wait."

Conner seemed unusually quiet as he and DJ exited the cafeteria. Of course, she didn't feel much like talking either. This news that guys could possibly be crashing their spring break was not the least bit welcome.

"Do you think they'll really come to Palm Beach?" she quietly asked Conner. "Or is Lane just full of it?"

"Who knows?" He shrugged and looked away.

"Are you okay?" She peered closely at him. "Did I say something to offend you?"

He turned and looked back. "Not exactly. But I guess it's not that cool to find out your girlfriend is going to pose for the *Sports Illustrated* swimsuit edition, not to mention partying with a bunch of hormone-driven boys during spring break."

DJ couldn't help but laugh. "For starters, it's *not Sports Illustrated*, Conner. It's a designer named Josie who's trying to launch her own line of swimwear. And with my grandmother there, well, you can count on the fact that the shoot will be respectable."

"I guess. But what about the guys?"

"What about them? For one thing, don't you think it's highly speculative that they'll even be able to come down there at all? And for another thing, Lane's grandparents' house might be miles from the general's. Besides that, what do I care?" She tucked her arm into his. "You're the only guy I'd want to hang with anyway."

He smiled. "Really?" She nodded.

"Because I know I've seen Lane looking at you, DJ. I can tell he thinks you're hot."

She laughed again. "I think he's only got eyes for Eliza now."

"Don't be too sure."

She scowled at him. "What difference would it make anyway? If I'm not into him, why would it even matter?"

"Because he's a guy."

"Don't be so paranoid."

He sighed. "I guess a part of me wishes I was going now."

"Me too. But I really respect you for staying here for the soccer playoffs, Conner. I wish I could stay too."

"Why don't you?"

She considered this. "For one thing, my grandmother would throw a fit." Then she looked at the cloudy sky overhead. "And for another thing, sunshine and warm sand are sounding pretty good."

He nodded. "I have to agree with you there."

"Hey, what if you came down *after* the playoffs, Conner? Aren't they in the middle of the week?"

He seemed to consider this. "Yeah, maybe I could fly down on Thursday. It would only be for a few days, but it'd be better than nothing."

She nodded with enthusiasm. "So think about it, okay?"

"I will." Then he frowned. "Except that ... "

"What?"

"Well, what if the guys turn it into a big booze party all week? I mean, it might be a total mess—a mess I'd just as soon avoid, you know?"

"Talk to Lane about it. See what he says. You'd think he'd want to be respectful of his grandparents' home—if he really is their favorite."

"You'd think."

"Why don't you come with us?" DJ persisted as she was driving Casey home after their soccer match on Saturday. She was trying to talk Casey into joining her and Taylor for some quick afternoon shopping.

"Because I don't want to," snapped Casey.

"Well, I don't really want to either." DJ laughed. "You'll be in good company."

"Right. You and Taylor and me."

"What's wrong with that?"

"Nothing." Casey looked out the passenger's side window.

"Really, Casey, what's wrong? It's like you hate Taylor."

"I don't hate her. I just don't like her."

"Why not?"

"Man, do I need a reason? She's been a total witch and she—"

"Since when has she been a total witch?" DJ slowed down for the stoplight.

"You know."

"No, I don't know." She turned and looked at Casey. "Seriously, I don't know. Why are you turning on Taylor?"

"Because she and Eliza are the same."

"The same?" DJ could hear her voice getting louder.

"And I don't know why you're always defending her—like you and she are best friends. And just because she claims she's a Christian, which I frankly doubt."

"You doubt her faith?"

"She's just trying to make you like her."

"Casey!" The light turned green and DJ pulled out. "That's nuts!"

"And now you think I'm nuts."

"No, not you. But that you'd think such mean things about Taylor. It's like you don't even know her."

"And you do?"

DJ nodded. "Yes. I do."

"It's like she's got you under her spell. She's made you believe that she's changed. But she hasn't. She's just the same. She's a witch."

"Casey, I can't believe how mean you're being."

"I'm being mean?"

"Yes."

"She's the one who was flirting with Seth during chemistry yesterday. Just because I asked him to the dance, she suddenly thinks she can take him back. It's like she wants to show me who's boss."

"Oh, I seriously doubt—"

"See! That just proves how gullible you are, DJ."

"But Taylor has no interest in Seth."

"Right, he's her cast-off." Casey's voice was dripping in sarcasm now. "Why would Taylor want Seth back? Let *poor little Casey* pick up Taylor's hand-me-downs. But just make sure Casey knows that Taylor could get him back if she wants—anytime she wants."

"Oh, Casey, that's not fair."

"No, it's not fair. But that's what Taylor is, DJ. You may be blind to her faults, but they're still there. She wants every guy to bow down to her—she gets her highs out of seeing them on their knees and—"

"Casey!" DJ glanced sharply at her friend.

"Fine. I'll shut up. I knew you wouldn't listen anyway. You always take her side."

Fortunately they were home now. And, although DJ wished for more patience, she had just about had it with Casey and her fits of jealousy today. It was one thing for Casey to take it out on DJ on the soccer field, which she had done when DJ had rescued Casey's fumble and managed to salvage a last-second score. But to lash into Taylor when she wasn't even around to defend herself was just too much. Casey really needed to get over herself!

"I'll take that as a no then," DJ said lightly to Casey as they walked into the house. "That you'd rather not go shopping with Taylor and me today."

As if to seal the deal, Casey swore just in time for Inez to overhear her.

"Casey Atwood!" Inez sternly shook a finger in Casey's face. "Watch your language."

"Sorry," Casey muttered as she ran upstairs.

DJ gave Inez a sympathetic half-smile, then slowly followed her foulmouthed friend up the stairs. Lovely, just lovely.

"Hey, I was just wondering if you'd changed your mind," Taylor said as DJ entered the room. "I tried to call you, but your phone must be off. I was about to dust off my Vespa and . . ." She paused to look at DJ. "Is something wrong?"

DJ shrugged. "Just Casey. She's in a snit."

"Bad game?"

"Not really. I think Casey's just having P.M.S. or something."

"Does she want to come with us?"

DJ kind of laughed. "I don't think so."

"Do you want to get ready or are you going like that?"

DJ looked down at her sweats. "I suppose I could spiff up a bit."

"Ya think?" Taylor laughed. "I'll be downstairs."

DJ hurriedly changed into her good jeans, boots, and a brown leather jacket that she knew Taylor liked. Then she fluffed out her hair, put on a bit of mascara and lip gloss, and called it good enough. It wasn't that she didn't care about her appearance. She just didn't care as much as some people. Still, she knew that it wouldn't hurt to make a little bit more of an effort. Plus, it might keep Grandmother off her case.

"I wish I could go with you girls," Grandmother was saying to Taylor downstairs.

"Why don't you?" suggested Taylor.

"Oh, I'm meeting the general at three." Grandmother feigned disappointment, but DJ could tell she was actually relieved. "I'm afraid I'll have to do my beach tog shopping next week while you girls are in school."

"Less crowded then," said DJ.

Grandmother nodded. "Yes. Now, you girls have fun. And Taylor, don't you let DJ come home empty-handed."

Taylor laughed as they headed out the door. "Don't worry, I won't."

"I'm sure I must be one of the few teenage girls on the planet that has to be encouraged to shop."

"Unless you're buying sportswear, anyway."

"Come to think of it, I could use a new—"

"No way." Taylor gave DJ a gentle shove toward the car. "Forget about going to any sporting goods stores."

"Hey, I'm the driver." DJ pushed the button to unlock her car.

"But I'm buying your gas."

"You are?"

"Sure."

"And lunch?"

Taylor laughed. "If that's what it takes to keep this shopping trip on track, yes."

"Okay, I'm starving."

"And that's something new?"

DJ patted her stomach. "Just one of the many benefits of doing sports, Taylor. You should try it sometime."

"I used to do sports ..." Taylor leaned back in the seat and yawned lazily. "But then I realized that I didn't particularly enjoy sweating."

"But you do some kind of exercise." DJ glanced at her sleek roommate and wondered. "Don't you?"

"A little yoga here, a little Pilates there ... it all seems to work out. At least, I haven't heard any complaints. Have you?"

"Yeah, right. People come up to me all the time saying, 'That Taylor, she's such a wreck.'"

Taylor laughed loudly and then the car got quiet. DJ was still thinking about Casey and wondering if any of what she said could possibly be true.

"Something wrong?" Taylor asked after a few minutes.

"I was just thinking about Casey ... trying to figure her out."

"And?"

"And I can't."

"What about your P.M.S. theory?"

"I think it's more than that."

"Like what?"

DJ sighed. "Like jealousy."

"Oh ..." Taylor nodded in a knowing sort of way. "Is Casey jealous of you?"

"Not me."

"Who then?"

"Maybe you."

"Seriously?" Taylor sounded surprised.

"I know I probably shouldn't have told you. You won't say anything, will you?"

"Of course not. But why on earth would Casey be jealous of me?"

DJ gave a short laugh. "I can think of a few reasons. In fact, I'm sure there are a lot of girls who are jealous of you."

"Like who?" Taylor's voice sounded a little bit catty now, like she was enjoying this.

"Like Eliza for starters."

"Oh, well, Eliza is jealous of anyone who takes one tiny beam of limelight away from her glittering stage."

"And there are girls at school ... you know, like Madison and Tina."

"Madison and Tina are jealous of all the Carter House girls."

"Well, maybe."

"Seriously, why would Casey be jealous of me?"

"I think she's worried about Seth."

"She *should* be worried about Seth."

DJ felt slightly alarmed. Was Casey right? Maybe Taylor really was up to something in regard to Seth. "Why?"

"Because Seth is bad news."

"Well, yeah, that's what I think too. But what do you mean specifically?"

"I mean, you can't trust him. Oh, he's great at looking good and acting sweet and innocent, and he's very smooth, but underneath it all he's after only one thing."

"Meaning?"

"You know exactly what I mean, DJ."

"Sex?"

"Duh."

"But don't you think Casey knows that?"

"I don't know. I mean, Casey tries to act all tough and street smart, but I'm not so sure that it's not just that—an act, I mean."

DJ nodded. "Yeah, I've wondered the same thing."

"But Seth might not see it that way. He might just assume that Casey is like him. In fact, I'm willing to bet that's what he thinks."

"Really? How can you be so sure?"

"I can see it in his eyes."

"So what makes Seth different than, say, Harry or Garrison?"

"It's hard to explain, but there's a difference. For sure, Harry and Garrison aren't angels. But they do know how to take no for an answer, if you know what I mean."

DJ nodded. "So are you saying that Seth didn't take no for an answer from you?"

"He gave it his best shot, but he didn't know what he was up against. Once I set him straight, it got better. But it still wasn't easy. And, as you know, I'm not exactly a pushover."

"Well . . . unless alcohol was involved."

Taylor didn't say anything.

"Sorry."

"No, that's a good point. But even then I sometimes had to draw the line with that boy. I sent him packing more than a couple of times."

"Do you think we should warn Casey?"

"I think someone should. But I'm just not sure she'll listen to me if she really is jealous."

"Which seems to be the case."

"She might assume I'm setting up some kind of smoke-screen, you know, so I can get old Seth-boy back." Taylor laughed. "Like I'd want him back. Puh-leeze. I mean, when I was drinking, he could be a kick. Nowadays, I think he'd be just a great big pain in the . . ."

"So . . . do you think I should tell Casey about him?"

"Do you seriously think she'd listen to you?"

DJ thought for a moment. "Probably not."

"She might listen to Rhiannon," Taylor said suddenly.

DJ nodded. "You know, I think she might. In fact, I'll bet that part of her attitude problem is that she's missing being Rhiannon's roommate."

"Well, before she starts planning her pity party, she should remember that Rhiannon's got her own problems with Eliza."

"Can you believe they went shopping together today?" The irony of this hit DJ. "I mean, can you imagine Rhiannon dragging Eliza into one of her second-hand shops? Forcing her to look at old shoes that have been worn by someone else?"

Taylor laughed. "Or our penny-pincher Rhiannon being forced to watch Eliza trying on five hundred dollar bikinis?"

"Five hundred dollars for a bikini? You gotta be kidding!"

"Well, that might be a little over the top. But four hundred dollars for a top designer wouldn't be surprising."

"That is so sad." DJ shook her head to think of what Rhiannon might do with four hundred dollars. And, really, it was sad to think that Eliza would have no problem plunking down that much cash—make that plastic—for a few scraps of fabric and strings. More and more, DJ respected Rhiannon's interest in frugal fashion. Too bad everyone didn't see the sensibility of just saying no to ridiculous designer price tags.

5

spring breakdown

"I already *have* swimsuits," DJ said as Taylor held up a skimpy red bikini.

"You don't have this one." Taylor waggled the stringy pieces back and forth as if she were tempting DJ—which she wasn't.

"I don't want *that* one."

Taylor made a face then added the bikini to her own pile. "Fine, I'll try it on and then you'll be sorry."

"I doubt it."

"Please don't tell me you're planning on wearing your swim team suits in Palm Beach," teased Taylor.

"I might." DJ fingered through the swimsuit rack until she found a navy one-piece that was actually pretty cute. "How about this?" She held it up and Taylor's brow creased in disapproval.

"Looks like something your grandmother might wear."

DJ held up the suit and frowned. "I think it's cut a little low for her, uh, sagging cleavage."

Taylor laughed. "You could be right. And, who knows, it might look good on you. Why don't you try it?" She shoved another one-piece toward DJ. "And try this one too."

DJ laughed. "Zebra stripes? I don't think so."

"Give it a shot, okay? And this one too." The next one-piece was slate colored with silver metallic rings holding it together. Before long DJ had quite an assortment of one-piece suits. But once they were in the fitting room, Taylor insisted on seeing DJ in a bikini.

"What are you afraid of?" Taylor asked as DJ modeled a skimpy bikini.

"You mean besides losing my top or bottom if I go swimming?"

Taylor laughed. "It's not really made for swimming."

"But I like to swim. And I like to move around. And, unlike some girls, I don't like parts of my anatomy hanging out while I'm moving."

"You're such a prude."

DJ frowned. "Well, think about it, Taylor. I mean, you're a Christian. What do you suppose God thinks about us running around practically naked? And, if Lane's plan for getting his grandparents' house pans out, there will be guys around."

Taylor grew thoughtful. "So, what are you saying?"

"I'm saying that wearing this"—DJ pointed down to the small triangles of fabric that barely covered her private parts—"is kind of like waving a red flag in front of a bull—or in other words it's like waving a naked girl in front of a hormonal teenaged guy. It might spell trouble."

"Sometimes you remind me of an old woman." Taylor sighed. "Honestly, don't you ever want to ... you know ... with Conner?"

"Of course." DJ laughed. "I'm human and so is he."

"So what keeps you from ... going there?"

"We have an agreement." DJ wondered how much she should say and whether Conner would mind.

"An agreement?"

"Well, we've had some times when things got a little too hot and heavy."

"Like the night at the fleabag motel in Vermont?"

"No." DJ made a face. "We were both pretty creeped out by that sleazy place, and it was, you know ... "

"Unromantic."

"Totally."

"So?" Taylor reached for another bikini. "It sounds like you guys never went too far. I don't get it."

"You might not remember, but Conner and I quit dating for a while—"

"I remember you broke up, but there was the Haley factor."

"To start with we broke up mostly because we were worried that our relationship was going to compromise our convictions—it was pretty mutual."

Taylor's eyes lit up. "Meaning you both *wanted* to have sex?"

"I don't know that we wanted it—not like it was all pre-planned and agreed on—but, yeah, when things went too far, we both probably wanted it. It was a temptation."

Taylor's expression grew skeptical. "But you and Conner both have so much self-control."

"Maybe ... " DJ considered this. "But why push it? Why set yourself up? I mean, you wouldn't bring a bottle of vodka to our room and just set it on your bedside table to prove you had self-control, would you?"

Taylor laughed. "Yeah, right."

DJ pointed to Taylor's bikini again. "I guess that's my point."

Taylor thrust her ample chest out and struck a pose in front of the mirror. "You think I'm trying to flag down guys, begging them to come jump my bones?"

"Sorry, but I'm just being honest. That's kinda how I see it."

Taylor studied her reflection with a more thoughtful expression. "But you could be right."

DJ brightened. "Really?"

Taylor flipped a string of DJ's bikini top, causing it to slip down. "I suppose this is kind of like baiting the hook, like we're trying to reel them into bed. And I, for one, am not."

"Me neither."

"Maybe I'll look for some more conservative bikinis."

"Is there such a thing?"

"I saw some DKNY pieces that aren't quite so revealing. And who knows, they might even look classy."

"And if it's all the same to you, I'm sticking with the one-piece numbers."

"To be honest, you looked really hot in that one with the rings."

"I actually liked it too."

And so by the end of the shopping afternoon, they had managed to accumulate some new swimwear that could actually function in water as well as some shorts and tops and sandals. Although DJ's choices were far less expensive than Taylor's designer choices, she was perfectly happy with them. And even if her grandmother wasn't impressed, DJ thought she should appreciate the fact that DJ had saved her a few bucks on her credit card.

DJ had barely pulled into the driveway before Eliza's little white Porsche pulled up behind them.

"Perfect timing," Taylor said with sarcasm.

"Hey, y'all," called out Eliza as she emerged from her car with about a dozen shiny shopping bags hanging from her like appendages. "Have any luck shopping?"

Taylor held up her bags as if they were proof. "We did okay."

"I found some real treasures," said Rhiannon as she pulled a motley-looking bunch of bags from the back of the car. "I can't wait to see what you guys think of them."

"Let's go inside and have show and tell," said Eliza in an excited voice.

Taylor made a smirk, which Eliza fortunately didn't see.

"That's a great idea," said Rhiannon. "You guys want to come to our room?"

So the four girls and their bags crammed into Eliza and Rhiannon's room to show what they'd purchased. Naturally, Eliza made fun of DJ's one-piece swimsuits. And, in return, DJ made fun of Eliza's outrageous price tags.

"I cannot believe anyone in her right mind would pay two hundred and fifty dollars for this." DJ held up the lacey pink bikini and just shook her head.

"It happens to be a Dolce and Gabbana." Eliza said this as if it explained everything.

"I thought D and G only made purses." DJ set the skimpy swimwear back down in the tissue paper.

"That shows how little you know about fashion." Eliza nodded to Rhiannon. "Even Rhiannon knows better than that."

"What do you mean, 'Even Rhiannon'?" Rhiannon demanded.

"Sorry, that came out wrong." Eliza put a finger to her lips. "I meant that even though you don't buy the big designers, you still know who they are and what they do. Right?"

Rhiannon smiled now. "Absolutely. It's part of my education."

"Look what I got for our little designer girl," said Eliza as she pulled out a leopard-print bikini. "Isn't it adorable? It's a D and G too."

"You got that for me?" Rhiannon looked stunned. "I didn't know—"

"It was so great on you," gushed Eliza. "You looked totally hot."

"Wow." Rhiannon fingered the fabric and sighed. "Thanks, Eliza."

"See, it pays to shop with Eliza." She tossed a smug look to Taylor and DJ. Like they'd even care.

"Show us what you got for our Rockabilly outfits," said Taylor suddenly. "Did you find any boots?"

"I actually marked some things on eBay and a couple other retro sites, but I want you guys to look at them and, of course, you'll need to bring your credit cards. They have some pretty good deals, and we'll need to act fast if we want them shipped in time for the dance. But at least they'll be broken in since they've been previously worn."

"*Used* footwear?" Eliza made a face. "I don't think so."

"They're retro," said Rhiannon. "And it's not easy finding new cowboy boots with the kind of character that these old collectable ones have."

"Does character come with anti-fungal foot powder?" asked Eliza.

DJ couldn't help but laugh. "I'll bet they might throw that in for free if you asked nicely."

"Or throw it at you," added Taylor.

"Fine," said Rhiannon, "get your boots new if you want, Eliza. But if you find anything as cool as the ones I found, you might end up paying a thousand bucks for them."

Eliza just shrugged. "So?"

"You're willing to throw away a thousand bucks for a pair of boots that you'll only wear like once?" demanded DJ.

"I might wear them more than once." Eliza held her head up. "And if I don't, I can always donate them to a good cause."

"If my feet were bigger, I'd volunteer to be your good cause," said Rhiannon.

Then Rhiannon showed them some of her shopping finds. Although her bargain pieces of plaids and polka dots and bandanas and old belts and buckles and things didn't really look like much to DJ. She tried to act interested as she wondered how Rhiannon would possibly pull this off. And yet, she'd seen Rhiannon turn rags into riches before so she wasn't really worried.

"You're amazing," she said to Rhiannon finally. "I mean, you look at a bunch of, well, junk and you see cool clothes. Whereas I look at a bunch of junk . . . and that's all I see."

"Just give me a few days and you'll see cool clothes too."

"Now, let's see what you girls got." Eliza turned her focus onto Taylor and DJ.

"I doubt you'll be too impressed with my shopping." DJ dumped her bags out onto Rhiannon's bed. And, just as she thought, Eliza was unimpressed. "What's with these boring one-piece suits, DJ? You might as well have just gone with your swim team suits."

DJ laughed as she dropped them back into the bags. "That's exactly what I said, but Taylor thought I could do better."

"And she actually looks great in those suits," Taylor defended her. "Sometimes sexy is subtle."

"Okay, *Sexy*," said Eliza, "show us what you got."

Taylor casually pulled out item after item, and while Rhiannon gushed and oohed over Taylor's great sense of style and taste, Eliza just looked blankly on — as if she were bored. Although DJ was pretty sure that Eliza was impressed. She just didn't want Taylor to know.

"So," said Taylor as she put her purchases back in her bags, "thus ends show and tell. Thank you, ladies."

"Maybe we can get together to check out the boots later," said Rhiannon.

"I have a date," Taylor told her. "But maybe I could pick out some boots before I go, okay?"

"Okay."

"A date with Harry?" asked Eliza with way too much interest.

Taylor looked evenly at her. "Does it really matter?"

Eliza shrugged. "I guess a girl who's willing to wear hand-me-down boots shouldn't mind a hand-me-down boyfriend."

Taylor laughed. "Since Harry broke up with you, I would think you'd be considered the hand-me-down — I mean, if there is such a thing."

"Hand-me-downs, sloppy seconds . . . call it what you like. But just don't forget I had him first, Taylor."

"Really?" Taylor cocked her head slightly. "Meaning you were Harry's very first girlfriend?"

"You know what I mean."

Taylor had her bags gathered up now. "Oh, yeah, Eliza, I know what you mean. But I do think you should get over it, okay? It's not good to hold onto guys once they've moved on, you know?" Then Taylor exited before Eliza could respond.

"Wow," said DJ once they were in their room. "That was starting to sound like a catfight."

"Oh, I wouldn't stoop that low." Taylor tossed her bags onto her bed and kicked off her high-heeled short boots. "In fact, I wish I hadn't stooped at all." She sank down on the bed and sighed. "But Eliza just gets my goat sometimes."

"And you think you don't get hers?"

Taylor smiled. "Oh, yeah, I know I do."

"You actually enjoy it, don't you?"

"I'm not sure what Jesus would do, but maybe Eliza needs someone to put her in her place from time to time."

"Do you think Jesus would put her in place *with love*?"

Taylor laughed. "That's an interesting concept."

Just then there was a tapping on the door and DJ opened it to see Rhiannon with her laptop. "Ready to do some boot shopping?"

Soon they were looking at funky old cowboy boots, and before long they'd each picked out a pair and locked in their purchases.

"Guess that's it," said Rhiannon, but she didn't leave.

"Everything going okay?" asked DJ tentatively.

Rhiannon shrugged. "I guess so ... "

"You seem kind of down," persisted DJ. "Is something wrong?"

"It's Eliza."

"Big surprise there," called Taylor from the bathroom. "We were just wondering how you've put up with her this long." She popped her head out and looked sympathetic.

"That's not it," Rhiannon said quickly. "The truth is Eliza's been pretty nice to me. Especially lately."

"Really?" Taylor emerged from the bathroom with a creased brow. "Sometimes you need to keep your guard up when someone like Eliza is being nice to you."

"I don't think so." Rhiannon looked at DJ. "In fact, I think Eliza gets tired of you guys picking on her so much."

DJ pointed to her chest. "Me? She thinks I pick on her?"

"You both do. And so does Casey."

"Casey picks on everyone," DJ tossed back.

"You might be surprised to hear that Casey and Seth are going out with Eliza and Lane tonight."

"That should be interesting," admitted DJ.

"Anyway, I can't tell you what to do, but I'm trying to be nicer to Eliza and I wish you and Taylor would too."

Taylor leaned against the doorframe, folding her arms across her chest, just waiting for Rhiannon to continue.

"I know Eliza can be, well, kind of a snob," she said. "But underneath that . . . she's okay."

"So what are you saying?" Taylor asked.

"Just that . . . you guys are both Christians . . . and maybe you should try being nicer to her."

DJ shrugged. "Yeah, maybe. We were actually just talking about that. Sort of."

Rhiannon brightened. "Good. I thought you'd understand."

Taylor's mouth twisted into a half-smile. "This could be a challenge, but it might be kind of fun too."

"Thanks, you guys." Rhiannon stood now. "I don't think you'll be sorry either. I mean, it's not like getting into fights is fun, right?"

"I don't know." Taylor chuckled. "I used to kind of enjoy it."

"But that was the old you," Rhiannon reminded her. "God's at work in the new you. Remember."

"I'll try." Taylor looked at the clock by her bed. "In the meantime I'd better get ready. Harry will be here soon."

DJ thought about what Rhiannon had said while Taylor was getting ready for her date. It actually made sense. Not that it would be easy being nice to Eliza. But it was probably the right thing to do. And who knew . . . maybe in time Eliza would change. After all, Taylor had changed—was still changing. And so was DJ. So miracles could still happen.

6

spring breakdown

"Harry and I are going to host a dinner before the Rockabilly dance," Taylor announced at the breakfast table on Tuesday morning. "Naturally, you're all invited."

"Naturally," Eliza repeated in a saccharine tone.

Taylor's eyes narrowed ever so slightly as she smiled at Eliza. "It'll be at the beach house."

"Sort of a repeat of the dinner party we had before the Winter Ball?" Eliza ventured.

"Except for one thing." Taylor looked directly at Grandmother now. "There will be no alcohol served."

"Goodness!" Grandmother looked shocked. "Was alcohol served at the other dinner party?"

Everyone got very quiet.

"As a matter of fact, there was," Taylor continued carefully. "But that won't be happening this time. Harry and I will make sure of it."

Grandmother sighed. "Well, that's a relief. I'd hate to think that any of my girls are participating in underage drinking."

"And if anyone brings alcohol to the dinner party"—Taylor looked directly at Eliza now—"it will be confiscated and disposed of."

Eliza put on her most innocent face. "Well, of course it will. Not that any of our friends would do something like that."

"No," Taylor nodded. "I'm sure they wouldn't."

Thanks to Rhiannon, the conversation now shifted to dance clothes. Her plan was to have everyone try their outfits on Wednesday night. "I'll have to miss youth group," she said. "But there's really no other way to get this done. We'll have a fitting and then I can do my final alterations on Thursday after school," she told them.

"And I've decided to go with a slightly different rockabilly style," Eliza said. "Actually, it's more authentic than what Rhiannon's putting together."

Rhiannon sort of rolled her eyes. "It depends on how you define authentic, Eliza." Then she smiled. "But if you want to look like Marilyn Monroe goes country, I'm okay with it."

Eliza laughed. "I happen to think Marilyn Monroe is hot."

"This will be such fun," said Grandmother happily. "I love seeing you girls all dressed up for these little events. Maybe I should invite the general to come with his camera again."

The plans continued and before long it was time to head to school.

"That was brilliant," DJ told Taylor as they drove to school.

"What was brilliant?" asked Casey from the backseat.

"Banning alcohol from the dinner party."

"Oh."

"Thanks." Taylor put on her shades. "I figured we'd just nip this thing in the bud. A preemptive strike."

Casey laughed. "You seriously think Harry can keep the other guys from bringing booze?"

"Conner and Harry will talk to them," said DJ. And although she hadn't mentioned this to Conner, she knew she could count on him.

"And I think Rhiannon can convince Bradford to climb on the wagon," Taylor continued. "He's never been a big boozer anyway."

"And I'm pretty sure that Josh only drinks to be social," added DJ.

"Meaning that just leaves Seth and Lane?" asked Casey.

"Pretty much." Taylor turned around to look at Casey. "I'm sure you don't want Seth to drink, Casey."

"What makes you so sure?" Casey's tone was sharp now, almost like a challenge.

"For your sake, I don't think you'd like to have Seth drinking."

"Remember what happened with Garrison," DJ reminded her. "Going to the Winter Ball in a barf-soaked dress wasn't too—"

"In case you forgot, I never made it to the dance."

"Just my point, Casey," persisted DJ. "Why go back there again?"

"I've never seen Seth wasted like that."

"Trust me," said Taylor, "you don't want to."

That shut Casey up, but DJ could tell that she was fuming. And as soon as the car was parked at school, Casey grabbed her stuff, jumped out, and took off.

"Guess I stepped on her toes," said Taylor as she slung a strap of her bag over her shoulder.

"I don't know why she's being so hypersensitive."

"Probably because she's a little insecure," said Taylor evenly, "and because she feels things deeply."

DJ considered this. Taylor was right. Casey was insecure and she did take things hard. But what good did it do her in the long run? She usually just ended up hurting herself as well as those around her. "Casey needs God in her life," stated

DJ as they went into the school. "*That* would make a huge difference."

"Amen, sister!" Taylor gave DJ a high five and laughed.

It wasn't that DJ hadn't been praying for Casey. And DJ sometimes tried to share her faith with her. But Casey usually acted like she knew it all, like she'd heard it before. After all, Casey had been raised in a "Christian home." Never mind that her parents fought like they wanted to kill each other sometimes. But Casey wasn't exactly open to listening to anyone talk about God. Plus, she continued to question Taylor's sincerity. In some ways, Casey seemed like she was the on path to fall flat on her face . . . but maybe that would get her attention and help her to rethink some things. DJ hoped so.

But DJ wasn't prepared for how Casey suddenly seemed to be aligning herself with Eliza. It just made no sense. In so many ways, Eliza was everything that Casey claimed to hate—superficial, materialistic, stuck-up, and insincere. DJ had even heard Casey refer to her as "plastic." And yet, there was Casey, sitting next to Eliza at the lunch table, laughing together like they were the best of friends. It felt even weirder when DJ saw Rhiannon joining in—like the three of them were the new It group, surrounded by several guys and enjoying the attention. Kriti was there too, although she had her nose stuck in a book. But the really odd thing was that no one had saved DJ a seat.

DJ glanced around, looking for Taylor, and saw her just coming into the cafeteria. She waved and together they found empty seats at a nearby table.

"This is different," said Taylor as they sat down. "Are we being shunned or something?"

"I don't know. But it seemed a little weird to me."

"I'm sure we could've forced our way in, but this might be more interesting." Taylor nodded toward the table where Eliza was keeping her little audience of girls and guys entertained with a story about what she'd done for spring break last year. It seemed she was speaking loudly so that DJ and Taylor would be sure to notice, not to mention embellishing it for the sake of her listeners, but who could know for sure?

"She seems like she's up to something," observed Taylor.

"And that surprises you?" DJ opened a ketchup package and squirted it onto her burger.

"Hey, ladies," Harry called out as if he'd just noticed that Taylor and DJ were at another table. "What're you doing over there?"

Taylor just smiled. "Eating lunch … by ourselves."

He frowned. "Intentionally?"

Taylor pointed to the table. "No room over there."

Just then Conner showed up, taking the seat next to DJ. Within seconds their table filled up, and suddenly Taylor was the center of the conversation. DJ wasn't sure if Taylor was enjoying this attention or not, but she did notice that Eliza was watching. It felt like there was some kind of secret competition going on between the two girls.

"I've made it clear to everyone that our dinner party will not involve alcohol," Taylor was explaining to Harry.

"What kind of party is that?" asked Garrison.

DJ frowned at him. "A party where someone doesn't end up barfing on his date."

"Low blow," he said to her.

"Besides, you don't even have a date, old boy," Harry pointed out.

Garrison nodded over toward Haley and Daisy. Both girls had just joined their table and had been listening in with interest. "I might have a date." He winked at Daisy now. "But I heard that the girls are supposed to do the asking."

DJ wanted to tell Daisy to run for her life, but it was too late.

"Is that a hint?" Daisy asked him boldly.

He grinned at her. "Yeah, I can rockabilly with the best of them."

Now she looked perplexed, like maybe she was rethinking this.

"Come on, Daisy," he urged her. "It'll be fun."

"If you ask Garrison," Haley challenged her, "I'll ask Nick Jefferson."

Daisy's eyes gleamed like this was a dare. "Okay," she declared. "You better not embarrass me now, Garrison."

He waited, and DJ cringed to imagine how humiliated Daisy would be if he was just jerking her chain. Poor Daisy was still getting used to her new image since her transforming makeover. And DJ wasn't sure if the *inner* Daisy was really ready for the *outer* one. Fortunately, thanks to Daisy's continued interest in sports, Eliza had given up on trying to turn Daisy into her permanent patsy. But even so, Daisy had changed.

"Okay," Daisy continued. "Want to go to the dance with me, Garrison?"

His brows lifted in a flirty way. "Oh, yeah, I sure do."

"You should dress up like Daisy Mae," suggested Taylor.

"Daisy Mae?" Daisy looked confused.

"It's a rockabilly dance," Taylor pointed out.

"So?"

"Haven't you ever heard of Li'l Abner?" Taylor asked her.

As it turned out, most of them hadn't heard of the old classic comic strip, but Taylor borrowed Harry's laptop, clicked onto a website, and explained the hillbilly characters to everyone with so much dash and style that her audience quickly grew. Funny what it sometimes took to draw a crowd. "My dad was a big fan of Al Capp," she told them.

By now several others had abandoned Eliza's table and joined this other group, and Lane was looking on with interest. "Hey, I should tell my mom about this," he said with enthusiasm. "She's helping with decorations and stuff, so she might find some inspiration here."

"Wow, Daisy Mae is hot," said Garrison as he pointed to the blonde bombshell in skimpy clothes. "I think Taylor's right, Daisy." He pointed to his date. "You should go as Daisy Mae."

Lane nudged DJ. "You'd make a good Daisy Mae too."

Conner's brow creased. "Shouldn't you be saying that to Eliza?"

Lane just laughed. "Hey, it's a free country. A guy can look, can't he?"

"You can look," DJ said in a forced light tone, "but don't touch."

Conner laughed, but still looked slightly uncomfortable. "Yeah, that's right."

Lane grinned with an odd twinkle in his eye. "Hey, Conner, did I hear you're not joining us in Palm Beach next week?"

"Soccer playoffs." Conner tossed DJ a sympathetic look. "But I might try to make it by the end of the week." Then he turned to Lane. "If I'm still invited."

"Oh, sure," Lane said easily. "I don't back out of an offer." He glanced around the crowded table. "And for you guys who're thinking about the Rockabilly dance, you better get your tickets. I hear they might be sold out soon."

"Isn't he the best promoter?" said Eliza as she joined Lane, slipping her arm into his elbow possessively. "I'll bet your mama is proud of you."

He just laughed. "Come on, Liza Jane, we need to discuss how we're going to make you into a Daisy Mae in time for the dance."

"She'll need implants," Taylor whispered into DJ's ear as she pointed to the voluptuous Daisy Mae character on the website, "or maybe a set of falsies and a good push-up bra."

DJ laughed. But then she got it. So that's why Lane was suggesting that DJ could be Daisy Mae. The insinuation was rather irritating. But the first bell rang and the cafeteria began to empty out.

"That Lane is a real piece of work," Conner told DJ as he walked her halfway to her class. They stopped in the hall between the science and math departments. "Tell me you couldn't see that he was flirting with you."

"I think he flirts with everyone," DJ said lightly. "I've seen him hitting on Taylor too."

"Well, I don't trust him."

DJ just shrugged. "He's just a jerk, Conner. Don't let him get to you."

Then it was time to go. As DJ hurried to Botany, she felt conflicted. On one hand it was a little aggravating for Conner to be that possessive of her. On the other hand, it was kind of nice. But she felt that his concern about Lane was overblown. Seriously, why would Lane be that interested in her? And even if he was, she wasn't the least bit interested in him. Plus there was the Eliza factor. DJ had no intention of attracting that girl's jealousy—even if it was unfounded.

7

spring breakdown

Grandmother allowed Rhiannon to use the third story ballroom as her design boutique. It wasn't only the Carter House girls taking advantage of her creativity, but several other girls from school as well. By Thursday, the day before the dance, Rhiannon had managed to help put together outfits for about ten girls and several guys as well. She didn't make everything from scratch, but she had such a knack for putting bits and pieces together that it all seemed to work out and, for the most part, everyone was pleased. But DJ had been surprised when Casey had gone along with Eliza, choosing to get her outfit from a costume store in town. As it turned out, Eliza was footing the bill, so that explained part of it. But it still didn't explain Casey's sudden interest in Eliza.

"You're really making some money," DJ pointed out as she slipped another check into Rhiannon's cash bag (actually an old beaded evening bag that Rhiannon had given her to use). DJ was assisting Rhiannon in her little business venture by acting as "cashier."

"I know," Rhiannon told her as she continued running her sewing machine, stitching some kind of funky red trim along the edge of a skirt made from several bandanas. "It's so cool. I mean, I almost feel like I'm a real designer."

"You are a real designer," DJ pointed out. "You're designing clothes and being paid to do it. How much more real does it get?"

Rhiannon nodded as she removed the skirt and clipped the threads. "How's that?"

"Perfect," said Haley as she took the skirt and held it up. "Thanks, Rhiannon! And I agree with DJ, you are a real designer."

"How does this look?" called out Daisy as she emerged from the makeshift dressing room—several sheets suspended by a wire in a corner.

Taylor let out a hoot as she entered the room. "Daisy Kempton, you look just like Daisy Mae," she called out. "Except we need to work on that hair—it needs to be puffy and curly and will probably involve some backcombing and hairspray."

"You *do* look like Daisy Mae." DJ couldn't help but laugh at the red-and-white-spotted peasant blouse and tight red skirt with a jagged hem.

"But do I really go barefooted?" asked Daisy with concern.

"You could wear cowboy boots until you get to the dance," suggested Taylor. "But if you're going for the real thing, you should go barefoot. And you need red lipstick."

"Are you here to try on your outfit?" Rhiannon asked Taylor. "It's not quite ready, but I could—"

"It's okay," Taylor told her. "I just wanted to see how it's going." She lowered her voice as Daisy went back to change into her street clothes. "And I thought you'd be interested to hear that Eliza and Casey are trying on their outfits downstairs."

"How do they look?" asked Rhiannon with concern. DJ knew that her feelings had been hurt by them looking elsewhere for their dance clothes.

66

Taylor grinned. "Pretty lame."

Rhiannon looked relieved. "I guess I shouldn't gloat," she admitted. "But tell us about them."

"The only reason I know is because I wanted to borrow Kriti's biology book to do some last-minute studying for my final tomorrow. And when I went into her room, Casey and Eliza were there trying on their stuff." Taylor chuckled. "Eliza didn't appreciate the intrusion, but just so you know, I was very polite and I told them both that they looked great. Actually, I think I told them that they looked hot." She laughed. "And that's not untrue. They look like hookers from the fifties."

"And they think that's rockabilly?"

"I guess it's one kind of rockabilly, or at least that's what the salesman at the costume store told them." Taylor picked up a big belt buckle. "But I think it's hokey and I have a feeling Eliza is regretting not letting you design an outfit. Yours are superior by far."

"Thanks, Taylor." Rhiannon continued to sew. "Unfortunately, it's too late for me to help them."

"Looks like Eliza and Casey will have to go as rocka-hookers," said DJ. "I just hope they're not sorry." DJ was thinking more about Casey than Eliza. In some ways, Eliza was simply getting what she asked for. But Casey … well, that was different. For some reason she was being pulled into Eliza's game and DJ just hoped that Casey wasn't getting in over her head.

Before long, the room cleared out and it was just Rhiannon and DJ. "I'm kind of worried about Casey," DJ admitted as Rhiannon continued to sew.

"Yeah, me too." Rhiannon glanced up then turned her attention back to the sewing machine. "And I feel partly to blame because I gave her that 'we should be nicer to Eliza' speech too."

"Seems like she took it a little too seriously."

"Oh, rats!" Rhiannon stopped sewing and pulled out the piece and shook her head. "I sewed that on wrong."

"I should probably quit distracting you." DJ stepped away. "Besides, I need to study for a botany test anyway."

"Tell Taylor that you guys can come try on your outfits in … let's see … " She looked at her watch. "Is eleven too late?"

"That's pretty late for you, Rhiannon." DJ looked down at her hardworking redheaded friend and suddenly got worried. "Hey, what about your classes? Do you have time to study?"

Rhiannon just nodded as she used a tool to rip out a seam. "I'll be fine."

"Because you don't want your grades to — "

"I said I'll be fine!"

DJ took another step back and just looked at Rhiannon. She knew that making money was important to her, but school should be important too. Rhiannon had been hoping to go to a good design school. But wouldn't she need decent grades to do that? "Later," DJ called as she headed out. Hopefully, Rhiannon was right. Hopefully, she was fine.

The late-night fitting went well and both DJ and Taylor were pleased with Rhiannon's work. "Aren't you going to bed, Rhiannon?" DJ asked as she and Taylor started to leave.

"Not yet." Rhiannon was back at her sewing machine. "I have to finish this."

"Don't overdo it," Taylor warned.

"I'm fine," Rhiannon shot back in an irritated tone.

After Taylor and DJ left, DJ felt even more concerned. And, once they were back in their room, she voiced this to Taylor.

"I know." Taylor nodded. "I think she's working too hard."

"I mean, it's been a good distraction," DJ admitted. "I haven't heard her mention her mom once this past week."

"The good news is that the dance is tomorrow," Taylor pointed out. "And even if Rhiannon is exhausted by then, she'll have all of spring break to relax."

"Well, besides our little photo shoot."

"Your grandmother promised it was only a one-day thing."

"Let's hope so."

"Anyway, it won't do Rhiannon any good to worry about her." Taylor was rubbing cream onto her elbows now.

"But we can pray."

Taylor nodded as she put the cap back on the cream. "Exactly."

DJ wanted to ask Taylor if she ever wanted to pray together, but somehow DJ couldn't quite get the words out. Besides, she was sleepy. Maybe some other time.

Taylor had taken charge of ordering the food for the dinner party at Harry's family's beach house. And since they were unsure of the number of guests (it kept changing), she had eventually told the caterers to plan on twenty-four guests. "Does that sound okay?" she asked DJ after her final phone call on Friday morning.

"I guess it's better to have too much than too little."

"Precisely my thinking."

"And do we need any kind of a plan ... I mean, just in case someone tries to sneak in some booze?" asked DJ as she pulled into the school parking lot.

"Conner and Bradford promised to act as bouncers so that Harry and I can play hosts."

"And I can help them," offered DJ.

Taylor chuckled. "Yes, I can just imagine you flexing some muscle in your cute little rockabilly costume. They'll be sure to take you real seriously."

"I'll have on my cowboy boots," she pointed out. "I could really kick some ... booze-smuggling behind." She laughed. "Hopefully that won't be necessary."

By the end of the school day, it felt like the entire school was on some kind of a high. Classes were finished and spring break seemed to have broken out fully. Suddenly everyone was acting like they'd just been released from a long prison sentence. Carter House was no different as the girls rushed about putting together the final touches to their rockabilly outfits as well as packing their bags for tomorrow's travels to Florida. Taylor was helping with makeup, and since Rhiannon (their usual hair expert) was still doing some last-minute alterations, Grandmother had brought in her own hairdresser, Val, to help the girls with their hair. His makeshift salon was located in the library.

"So I hear you girls are going to do a swimsuit shoot down in Palm Beach," Val said as he rolled a section of DJ's bangs onto a hot roller. "Wish you needed a hairdresser down there. I adore Palm Beach."

"Did you mention that to my grandmother?"

Val laughed. "As a matter of fact, I did. And she turned me down flat."

"Too bad."

"Tell me about it. Poor Val stuck up here in Connecticut while you girls are down there living the life. I hear the general's house is amazing."

"Really?"

"Right on the beach, but it has a pool too. Sometimes I think I was born into the wrong family." He shook his head sadly as he rolled up another section of hair. "I feel like there's a poor little rich boy trapped inside of me. And that I just need to find those wealthy ancestors that forgot to leave me all their beautiful estates and money."

DJ laughed. "I think being rich is highly overrated."

He chuckled. "Yes, you're probably right." Now he lowered his voice. "It doesn't seem to make our rich little heiress very happy. That girl was in such a snit when I did her hair earlier."

"A snit?"

"Oh, I know I shouldn't gossip." He chuckled. "But I AM a hairdresser, what can I say? Anyway, I asked Miss Eliza about what she was wearing to the dance — you know, so I'd know what kind of a hairstyle she was going for. But, goodness, the girl was perfectly rude about the whole thing."

"Rude?"

He nodded as he began to unroll a hot roller that had apparently been on long enough. "Yes, it seems that Miss Eliza had hoped to ace the best-looking outfit at the dance, but somehow her efforts went sour and now she's not a very happy camper."

DJ laughed. "She had the chance to have a designer original and she passed."

"Yes, our little Rhiannon is quite the talent, isn't she?"

"She's been working really hard." DJ considered this. "She doesn't have any rich ancestors either."

"So, I suppose this is a good reminder that money does NOT buy happiness." He laughed. "Not that I wouldn't like to give it a shot sometime."

Val continued to rattle on about money and a friend of his who had just purchased a beautiful home in Martha's Vineyard, and how he'd been hinting for an invitation for weeks now. "At least I might have a chance of meeting someone wealthy up there," he said as he undid the final roller. "If you can't be born into money, there's always the possibility of marrying it."

DJ laughed as he brushed out her curls, fluffing them up and backcombing them until she looked like a bad imitation of an old western singer. "Now, remember I'm not the one wearing the hooker dress, okay?"

He nodded. "Oh, yeah, I was getting carried away." He pulled it back into a very full-looking ponytail. "How about this?" He fluffed out her bangs.

"Perfect!" she declared.

"And maybe Rhiannon can find you a nice big ribbon to tie it with."

"Thanks, Val," she told him. "Shall I assume that Grandmother is handling your tip too?"

He gave her a sly look. "I cannot tell a lie, she is. But here's a tip for you, Sweetheart."

"Huh?"

"Watch your backside."

"What?"

"You know I don't like to gossip, but I overheard Miss Eliza on her cell phone. And I don't know what she was planning, but it sounded suspicious and your name came up."

"Really?"

He nodded. "Like she was going to try to slip something past you and Taylor tonight."

DJ nodded back at him. "Thanks for the heads up."

"Don't say you heard it here."

"I won't."

DJ hurried back to her room, hoping she could tip off Taylor. But it seemed she'd already left. DJ knew that she and Harry had planned to head to the beach house early in order to get things set up. So DJ tried Taylor's cell and then told her about Val's warning.

"Thanks," Taylor told her. "We'll be on high alert."

"And I'll let you know if I snoop out anything around here."

"I'm sure it's just that they think they can sneak alcohol into the dinner party." Taylor didn't sound too concerned. "And we'll just deal with it."

The general was on hand to take photos of the girls. He seemed to enjoy their outfits—particularly Eliza and Casey's. "You girls remind me of something," he said as he snapped some cheesy-looking pinup type shots. "Something from back when I was a young man."

"Call girls?" DJ whispered to Rhiannon.

Rhiannon suppressed a giggle.

"What's so funny?" asked Casey as she sauntered over toward them.

"Everything," said DJ as she looked down at her lace-trimmed denim skirt and stuck out a pointy-toed cowboy boot. "I mean, look at us, we all look pretty crazy." She tried not to stare at the bulging bodice of Eliza's low-cut hot pink satin dress, but it did seem that some kind of "enhancing" was going on there. Not that DJ planned to mention this.

"Crazy good," said Rhiannon.

Just then Conner arrived, and DJ realized they needed to get moving if they were going to head off the booze smugglers at the dinner party. "See you guys soon," she called to the others as she and Conner left.

"You look great," she told him as she admired the red fitted rockabilly cowboy shirt. "Did Rhiannon find that shirt for you?"

"She did." He smiled as he opened the door of his pickup for her. "And you are looking mighty fine yourself, little lady."

He slapped the big buckle on his belt. "This actually belongs to my dad," he said proudly. "He won it one summer when he was out West working on his aunt's ranch."

"At a real rodeo?"

Conner nodded then tipped his straw cowboy hat. "And this hat was his too. I think it's practically an antique. Remind me to be careful with it."

"You might want to take it off if you do any actual bouncing tonight."

He chuckled as he started the engine. "Hopefully things won't get too out of hand."

DJ said a silent prayer as Conner drove toward the beach. More than anything, she hoped things wouldn't get out of hand too. For once, it would be nice just to enjoy a fun party without all the crud that some people felt came with the territory.

8
spring breakdown

As it turned out, things didn't get the least bit out of hand at the beach house. But that was just because Harry, Taylor, Conner, and DJ seemed to be the only ones to show up.

"Do you think something happened to them?" DJ asked Taylor when it was past seven and still no one else had come. "Like a car wreck or something?" The guys had already been outside checking out the road to make sure that no one's car had gotten stuck in the soft spot by the creek. But it looked like they were on their way back now.

Taylor frowned. "More like an Eliza wreck."

"Do you think she's somehow gotten everyone to boycott the dinner party just because we said no alcohol?"

"I don't know, but I'm going to find out." Taylor picked up her phone and called Eliza, holding out her phone so DJ could hear it going straight to voicemail. Taylor just shook her head. "I'll call Casey," she said as she punched more buttons.

"Let me try Rhiannon," said DJ quickly. She hit speed dial and waited.

"DJ," said Rhiannon in a relieved voice. "I was so sorry to hear what happened."

"What happened?" asked DJ.

"You know, about the dinner party getting canceled because of that whole plumbing disaster."

"What plumbing disaster?" DJ was eyeing Taylor now.

"You know, the bathroom pipe that burst and flooded the entire beach cabin with sewage. What a mess."

"Who told you that?"

There was a long pause. "Eliza ... "

"There is *no* plumbing problem, Rhiannon. Eliza flat-out lied to you."

"Oh."

Taylor looked mad now. "What is going on?" she hissed.

DJ quickly explained and Taylor looked even more upset. "So where are you guys anyway?" DJ asked Rhiannon.

"At Lane's house. He and Eliza threw some things together for everyone so we could have dinner. It's actually pretty nice."

"Yes, I'm sure they just *threw* them together too."

"You could be right. Where are you guys anyway?"

"We're at the beach house," DJ said stiffly. "With a whole lot of great-looking food and no one besides us to eat it."

Rhiannon sighed. "I'm sorry."

"So are you guys coming or not?"

"Well, we've already started eating, DJ. And I don't really see how we can make it all the way out to the beach house and back to town without being really late for the dance, and Lane said they won't let anyone in after nine."

"Big surprise there." DJ growled. "Have fun!"

"If it makes you feel any better, *it's not that fun.* Lane's parents are at the dance and the bar is open." Rhiannon sighed. "Wide open!"

"It figures."

"Yeah ... " Rhiannon's voice grew sad. "And I thought tonight was going to be different."

"Think again."

"I wish I was with you guys instead."

DJ could hear Bradford in the background, urging Rhiannon to hang up the phone and come dance. "We'll see you later," she told Rhiannon. "Hang in there."

DJ shut her phone and looked blankly at Taylor. "Eliza Wilton is such a—"

"What's up?" asked Conner as he and Harry joined them in the kitchen. DJ quickly explained and Harry looked seriously irked.

"They went to all that trouble just so they could drink?" Conner asked in disbelief. "Isn't that pretty extreme?"

"Not just so they could drink," Taylor said quietly. "Eliza did it to get back at me."

"Get back at you for what?"

Taylor smiled at Harry. "What do you think?"

He pointed to his chest.

"That and a bunch of other things," DJ added. "Eliza seems to think she's in competition with all of us. And she just seems to take it to new levels."

"I can't believe she'd do something so low." Harry shook his head. "That explains why Lane and Garrison aren't answering their phones."

"Sure, why would they?" Conner said with a frown. "Lane's over there handing out free booze. I'm sure they were more than happy to hear that your pipes had burst, Harry."

"I'd like to burst something." Harry shook his fist in the air.

"They say the best revenge is living well," Taylor said calmly. "I suggest we all just sit down and enjoy this lovely meal."

Harry took in a deep breath then grinned at Taylor. "I like your style."

DJ nodded. "She's right. We should be having a good time. Why let the jerks get to us?" She looked around the pretty room, lit with lots of candles and strings of cheerful white lights. Harry had some good bluegrass music playing to "get them into the rockabilly mood."

"That's the spirit," said Conner.

"And now we can eat at the table together," said Taylor. "Instead of buffet."

Taylor and DJ soon had the table set, and Harry and Conner played waiter by serving them from the big dishes. And before long, they were all seated around the table, eating some very good food, and DJ realized that they really were having fun.

"This is so much better then being around a bunch of loud drunks," DJ pointed out as Harry and Conner headed to the kitchen for their dessert.

"No barfing, no fighting, no breaking things," said Taylor.

"Or being hauled off to jail for underage drinking," called Harry from the kitchen.

"A much better way to live," Taylor said happily.

"Very refined," said Harry as he sat the girls' desserts in front of them.

"And lots more food for us." Conner chuckled as he put a giant-sized piece of cherry cobbler à la mode at his place.

"What'll we do with the leftovers?" asked DJ suddenly. "We can't even take them home since we fly out in the morning."

"My mom works at the soup kitchen on Saturdays," said Conner. "Maybe I can see if she can use them."

"Now I feel even better," said Taylor. "Not only did we miss out on our friends sneaking their booze in here, which I'm sure would've happened, but we're helping to feed the poor as well."

Once they had finished eating, cleaned things up, and stowed the food in the fridge (until Conner's mom could pick it up in the morning), they headed off to the dance. DJ wasn't that surprised to see that their friends hadn't arrived yet. But the four of them headed straight out to the dance floor and whooped it up with the best of them. The rockabilly dance was a regular hoedown and actually a lot of fun.

"I don't know why they don't have lots of rockabilly dances," DJ announced as they were taking a break by the refreshment bar. "Or maybe I'm just a redneck at heart."

"It's fun to lighten up and act silly sometimes," agreed Taylor. "Without drinking, I mean."

"Didn't I hear that no one was allowed in here after nine?" Harry glanced at his watch.

"That's what Rhiannon said," DJ told him.

"Looks like some of them are just getting in under the wire." He nodded toward the entrance and they all peered over to see Lane and Eliza coming in, with Rhiannon and Bradford trailing behind. Eliza's cheeks were flushed and she looked a little rumpled. But what really got DJ's attention was Rhiannon. She actually seemed to be staggering.

"Do you think Rhiannon's been drinking?" DJ whispered to Taylor.

Taylor just shook her head. "Looks like a distinct possibility."

DJ waved toward them, but either they didn't see her or had decided to ignore her. "I'm going to find out what's up," DJ said suddenly.

"Not me," said Taylor. "I don't trust myself to speak to Eliza just yet."

"That works for me," said Harry as he grabbed her hand. "Let's go do some more boot-scootin' boogie."

And then they were off.

"Do you mind?" DJ asked Conner. "Rhiannon doesn't look too good, and I'd like to know where Kriti and Casey are."

"I'm with you," he said firmly.

They cut through the crowd until they reached where the foursome was gathered on the sidelines and Rhiannon was just sitting down. "Hey," said DJ in what she hoped was a friendly voice, "you guys made it after all."

"Barely," snapped Eliza.

"Well, you don't seem very happy to be here." DJ peered at Eliza and then over to where Rhiannon was sitting slumped over like a sack of potatoes. "Is she okay?"

"She'll be fine," Bradford said quickly. "Just got a little car-sick coming over here."

"Because you were driving like a maniac," snarled Eliza. "I thought we'd all be killed."

"You would've been killed if you'd let Lane drive."

DJ looked at Lane now and it looked like his eyes were barely focused. He was loosening his string tie and leaning into the table like he might fall over any minute.

"We had a lovely evening," DJ said suddenly. "A really nice meal and good company, and just as we were leaving we got to watch the moon rising over the ocean." She smiled at Conner. "Really beautiful, wasn't it?"

He nodded. "And this dance is fun too, Lane. Thanks for telling us about it."

"No problem." His voice was slurred. But then he seemed to wake up. "But what about that plumbing problem? All that raw sewage at Harry's place. You guys didn't eat there, did you?"

DJ laughed and looked directly at Eliza. "No, there was no plumbing problem. Eliza just made that little story up."

Eliza looked away now.

"You made that up?" Now Lane looked confused. "And we trashed my parents' house when we could've been—"

"Trashing Harry's place?" Conner offered.

Lane made a crooked smile. "Something like that."

"Well, thanks to the absence of booze, Harry's place is in great shape," continued DJ. "And our dinner was delightful."

"We're sorry you couldn't come." Conner looked evenly at Bradford now. "As it turned out, we didn't even need your help."

"Apparently Rhiannon did." DJ put a hand on Rhiannon's head, and Rhiannon let out a low moan. "Are you okay?" DJ asked her again.

"I jus' wanna go home."

DJ turned to Bradford. "Did you give her something to drink?"

He looked sheepish.

"Have you been drinking too?" demanded Conner.

Bradford held his thumb and forefinger to show "a little."

DJ peered more closely at him. "Are you drunk too?"

"No," he said in a way that was convincing. "I only had one beer. And I only gave Rhiannon one screwdriver. But it was on an empty stomach, and then I think someone gave her another and I'm not sure how much vodka was involved."

DJ shook her finger in his face. "And if she's sick, it's your fault."

"I just wanted her to have some fun," he said defensively. "She's been so uptight and she works so hard, and I thought one little drink would—"

"Lead to another," finished Conner.

"And here's what you're going to do," DJ said firmly. "You're going to call a cab and you're going to see that Rhiannon gets home. I'm going to call and ask Inez to meet you at the door and to help Rhiannon to bed. And I know Inez will do that because she actually likes Rhiannon." She narrowed her eyes at Bradford. "I thought you did too!"

Conner had his phone out now. "I'm calling you a cab," he told Bradford. "DJ's right, man, you need to take her home."

"But we just got here."

Rhiannon let out a low moan.

"I don't care." DJ wanted to punch him. "You get her home or I'll tell my grandmother what you did tonight, and she'll call your parents, and—"

"Fine!" He turned and reached down for Rhiannon. "We're going."

"And you be nice to her," snapped DJ.

"That's right," added Conner. "Or you'll be sorry."

DJ turned to Eliza now. "To be honest, I really don't want to talk to you, but I am curious as to the whereabouts of your roommate. And Kriti too."

Eliza rolled her eyes. "Kriti and Josh left the party early. I haven't the slightest idea where they went ... probably a lecture."

DJ felt relieved for Kriti's sake. "They probably got fed up with you drunks and figured the dance wouldn't be any better."

"We're not drunks."

DJ decided not to argue. "Okay, then, what about Casey and Seth? Where are they?"

Eliza just shrugged. "I don't have the slightest." Now she turned back to Lane. "Come on," she told him. "If we're not on the dance floor, we'll never get picked for best costume."

She reached for his string tie. "And I told you to leave that on, Lane. You have to look perfect."

DJ couldn't control herself now. "Yes, by all means, make sure you look perfect. You've lied to your friends. You've been drinking. You helped to make Rhiannon sick. You left your boyfriend's house trashed. But by all means you must look perfect." DJ laughed. "Not that it's even a possibility, Eliza. I mean, seriously, have you looked in the mirror lately?"

Eliza looked slightly shocked, but she recovered quickly. She patted her hair and quickly put on some lip gloss, then dragged Lane out to the dance floor.

"I shouldn't have talked to her like that," DJ admitted as they walked back to join Taylor and Harry. "I mean, I'm sure that's not what Jesus would say. But I just felt so angry."

Conner chuckled. "I don't know. Jesus called the Pharisees white-washed sepulchers, and what you just said to Eliza was kind of along those same lines."

"Huh? What's a white-washed sepulcher?"

"It holds something dead, but to white-wash it would be like a cover-up, you know? Kind of like Eliza wanted to look all perfect and be admired and even win a prize when she's been acting like a perfect fool."

As it turned out, Eliza and Lane didn't win the costume prize. But not for lack of trying. But to DJ's surprised delight, Taylor and Harry won first prize. And since Rhiannon had designed their outfits, she figured that meant Rhiannon had won too.

"Way to go," DJ congratulated the winning couple. "I can't wait to tell Rhiannon."

"I know," agreed Taylor. "I thought of calling her, but figured she might prefer to hear about it in the morning." Taylor frowned. "And I'm kind of worried about Casey too."

"So am I," DJ admitted. "I tried her phone and it seems to be off."

"Let's hope she's okay." Taylor shook her head. "I know I'll be praying for her."

"Me too." DJ tried not to think about the creepy things Taylor had told her about Seth, and she tried not to think about Casey being under the influence. Really, all she could do for Casey was to pray—and to hope Casey might learn from all this and hopefully make better choices in the future. Unfortunately "the future" seemed way too close. The Carter House girls would fly into Palm Beach tomorrow evening and Lane and the other guys—except Conner—would arrive by train on Sunday afternoon. What might happen then was anyone's guess. But tonight was about fun and DJ knew she could think about this other business later.

9

spring breakdown

The breakfast table was noticeably thinned out the next morning. "It looks as if some of the girls are already on vacation," commented Grandmother.

DJ controlled herself from saying, "Or suffering from hangovers."

"I hope that everyone will be packed and ready to go in time for our flight this afternoon."

"I'm all packed," said Taylor as she refilled her coffee cup. "And I just went online to check the Palm Beach weather and it looked fabulous. Low eighties and mostly sunny."

"Sounds lovely." Grandmother looked up to see Inez coming into the dining room with a cordless phone in hand.

"Kriti's mother wants to speak to you," said Inez.

DJ and Taylor exchanged glances then listened.

"Good morning, Mrs. Nahid," Grandmother said cheerfully. But as she listened, her smile quickly faded. "Really, she did? Why, I had no idea." She waited again. "Is she absolutely certain?" Despite her recent Botox treatment, her brow creased ever so slightly. "Oh, I'm very sorry to hear that, Mrs. Nahid. I know Kriti will be missed. Thank you for calling. Oh, yes.

Thank you." Grandmother pushed the off button and turned to DJ. "Did you know that Kriti went home last night?"

DJ's eyes grew wide. "Is she okay? Did something happen?"

"Apparently *something* happened." Grandmother narrowed her eyes at DJ. "And I would like to get to the bottom of it. When did you last see Kriti?"

DJ thought for a moment. "Here at the house, right before Conner picked me up."

"So Kriti did not go to the dinner party at the Green's beach house?" Grandmother looked disturbed. "Was she not invited?"

"Of course she was invited, Mrs. Carter." Taylor glanced at DJ as if to ask how much they should say. DJ just shrugged. "Everyone was invited," continued Taylor.

"But Kriti didn't attend the dinner party?" persisted Grandmother. "Was there a reason, Taylor?"

"Here's what happened." DJ jumped in and told her grandmother the whole story. Or nearly the whole story. She left out some details, like how Rhiannon had come home early because she'd drunk too much. Taylor and DJ had checked on her last night and she'd seemed much better. DJ also didn't mention that Eliza must've come home quite late since she hadn't been in her room when they'd tucked Rhiannon in.

"So you two girls and Conner and Harry were the only ones to attend your dinner party?" Grandmother was still trying to absorb this.

"Yes." Taylor sighed. "It was disappointing at first, but we managed to have a good time."

"And why did Eliza tell the others that you had a plumbing disaster?"

"We have a couple of theories," DJ offered.

"They are?"

"Well, Eliza is still a little jealous that Harry likes Taylor." Grandmother shook her head in a dismal way.

"And it's possible that some of them weren't terribly happy that we'd made it very clear that there would be no alcohol allowed at our dinner party," Taylor finished for her.

"So was there alcohol at the other dinner party — the one hastily put together by our own dear Eliza?"

Both Taylor and DJ said nothing, but Grandmother seemed to get it. "I'll take that as a yes," she told them.

"This is disturbing." Grandmother picked up the phone then set it down. "I'm not sure what should be done."

"So did Kriti's mom say why she came home?" Suddenly DJ was curious. "Did something happen?"

"Mrs. Nahid said that Kriti had suddenly gotten a strong case of homesickness and her boyfriend kindly offered to drive her home. They got there quite late and the boyfriend slept on the couch. Naturally, Kriti's parents were quite shocked to discover them there in the morning."

"Naturally." DJ thought about Casey now. She had assumed that both Casey and Kriti had been in their room sleeping off the effects of too much partying. Now she wondered.

"But that is not all," continued Grandmother. "It seems that Kriti has decided to forgo our Palm Beach trip."

"She's not going?" DJ felt bad now. "Did her mom say why?"

"Only that Kriti is very tired from studying and wanted a week to rest at home."

"She has some hard classes," pointed out DJ.

"And she really does study," added Taylor. "I'm sure she'll ace all her classes."

"Maybe some of the other Carter House girls should imitate Kriti's good study habits." This seemed aimed at DJ.

"Well, I'm glad she's okay," said DJ. She set her napkin next to her plate and asked to be excused.

"Yes, and will you tell the other girls that I want to have a little meeting?" Grandmother looked at her watch. "In the living room at ten o'clock sharp."

Taylor asked to be excused too and they both hurried upstairs to check the status of the other girls. But when they knocked on the door to Casey and Kriti's room, no one answered. And when they went inside, they saw that both beds were empty and hadn't been slept in.

"Where's Casey?" asked DJ.

"Good question." Taylor pulled out her cell phone and DJ headed for Eliza and Rhiannon's room. Rhiannon was taking a shower, but Eliza was still sleeping.

"Time to get up, Party Girl," DJ said loudly as she nudged Eliza.

"Leave me alone," Eliza drawled back at her.

"Grandmother wants to see you," DJ said firmly. "She wants you downstairs by ten o'clock sharp."

"What time is it?" she asked groggily.

"It's nine thirty-five."

Eliza groaned and slowly sat up, rubbing her head like it hurt.

"Now that you're bright eyed and bushy tailed," teased Taylor, "maybe you can tell us where Casey is."

"She didn't answer her phone?" asked DJ.

Taylor shook her head then turned back to Eliza. "Do you know?"

"Of course not."

"You might be interested to know that Josh drove Kriti home last night. Apparently they didn't enjoy your dinner party very much," DJ told her. "Kriti's mom just called my grandmother."

"Does Mrs. Carter know about the party?"

Both Taylor and DJ nodded.

"Is she mad?" Eliza actually looked concerned as she pulled on a pair of velour warm-up pants.

"Of course she's mad," DJ said calmly. "Did you think she'd be happy?"

"And now Kriti has decided not to go to Palm Beach."

"Just because of our party?" Eliza shoved her feet into her furry slippers.

"What do you think?" DJ asked her. "Did it seem like Kriti and Josh were enjoying themselves?"

Eliza pushed her blonde hair back and leaned over like she wasn't feeling very well. "I don't know ... "

"Well, maybe you should think about it," Taylor said quietly. "Maybe you should take some responsibility for your actions. Lying to everyone so that you could host a drinking party has consequences, Eliza. And, trust me, I've been there and done that so it's not like I'm judging you. I'm just warning you ... you're on a bad trail. I've been there."

Eliza just nodded. Then Rhiannon emerged from the bathroom, toweling her hair and looking slightly better than she'd looked last night. "What's up?" she asked. And they filled her in on Kriti's mother's phone call.

"Poor Kriti." Rhiannon shook her head. "I could tell she was fed up with the whole thing last night. If only we'd been at your party, Taylor."

"Except Eliza messed that up," DJ pointed out.

"Yeah." Rhiannon frowned. "Thanks a lot, Eliza."

"Fine," said Eliza in a hurt tone. "You all hate me. I get it." Then she trudged into the bathroom.

"There's something else," DJ told Rhiannon. "Casey is missing."

Rhiannon's eyes grew big. "Missing?"

"I just left her a message," Taylor explained, "but she never came home last night."

"Did you try Seth's phone?" asked Rhiannon.

"Good idea." Taylor opened her phone and punched in his number, and the next thing she was talking to Seth. At first he seemed to be playing with her but then Taylor got tough. "Look, Seth, this has nothing to do with you and me—so get over yourself, okay? I just want to know where Casey is and that she's okay. And if you don't get her back to the house by ten o'clock you will have the cops out looking for you and I am so not kidding. Capiche?" Then she hung up. "What a jerk!"

"Way to go!" DJ gave her a high five.

"Anyway, Mrs. Carter is having a meeting at ten," Taylor told Rhiannon.

"Do you think she's going to cancel the trip?"

Taylor shrugged. "I wouldn't really blame her."

"I'd be surprised," DJ admitted. "She'll probably just lecture us, read the house rules, and tell us to act like ladies."

"That's all?" Rhiannon looked slightly disappointed.

"You know how she is." DJ sighed. "This Palm Beach trip isn't just a vacation, it's a modeling job. You seriously think my grandmother will pass up on that?"

"Yeah," agreed Taylor. "Then she'd have to pay back the travel expenses and I'm sure that wouldn't sit too well."

"You got that right."

"What will we do if Casey doesn't make it back in time for the meeting?" asked Rhiannon.

DJ considered this. "I guess all we can do is tell my grandmother the truth."

Rhiannon shook her fist at the closed bathroom door. "Thanks to Eliza!"

"You can't blame Eliza for everything," Taylor told them. "Casey made up her own mind."

"That's right!" Eliza pushed the door open as if she'd been listening the whole time. "It's not my fault that all this is happening and it's really mean to try to pin it all on me." Now she was crying. Or pretending to cry. DJ wasn't sure. "I try to be nice to you guys and all I get in return is grief." She let out a loud sob.

"Lying to everyone to keep them from coming to my dinner party is being nice?" Taylor questioned her.

"And spiking my drink on purpose is nice?" Rhiannon added.

"Eliza spiked your drink?"

Rhiannon nodded. "That's what Bradford told me. He said he saw you do it, Eliza."

"If he saw me, why did he let you drink it?" Eliza shot back at her then blew her nose on a tissue. "Shouldn't he take some blame too?"

"It's time to put on your big girl pants, Eliza." Taylor looked directly into her face. "Grow up and take some responsibility for your actions." Then Taylor turned around and walked out. DJ followed her.

By ten o'clock all the girls (except Kriti) were seated in the living room. Some, like Casey—who showed up just before ten—looked a little worse for wear, but all were sitting up straight and paying attention as Grandmother did exactly as DJ had predicted. First she lectured them on the dangers of drinking and drugs. She even told a story about a model who'd had a bad vodka habit that eventually led to cocaine. "Oh, she was such a beauty too." Grandmother sighed. "Selena had a very bright future—everyone loved her. Naturally, when her problems hindered her work, she was eventually let go from the agency. And then I heard a year or two later that she died poor and alone of a heroin overdose. So sad." Then she told the girls how she didn't want them to end up like poor Selena.

"And now as a reminder to you girls, I will once again read the Carter House Rules," she announced. "I expect you to honor these rules for as long as you remain under my care." DJ tried not to snooze as Grandmother laboriously read the rules.

"And finally," she said as she folded the sheet of rules and slipped it into her blazer pocket, "I've thought long and hard about whether or not we should proceed with our trip to Palm Beach. Frankly, you girls have me a bit worried." She paused to study the girls. "But I have decided to give you another chance. And I hope you will not disappoint me."

Everyone seemed to relax a bit now and Grandmother asked if they had any questions.

"I don't have a question, Grandmother," DJ said suddenly. "But there's something I think you should know." The room got quiet again and both Eliza and Casey looked uneasy.

"Yes, DJ? Go ahead."

"Some guys from school are planning to go to Palm Beach too."

Grandmother just smiled. "Well, isn't that a nice coincidence."

"And they may want to come by and visit," DJ continued.

"Well, that should be fun for you girls." Grandmother nodded in a very obtuse sort of way.

"They're staying at Lane's grandparents' house," continued DJ. "Remember Lane Harris is the one who hosted last night's party with Eliza."

"Did you say Lane Harris?" Grandmother looked interested.

"Yes." DJ was stumped now. What did she have to do to make Grandmother understand?

"Is that Norman Harris's son?"

"That's right," Eliza said quickly. "Lane's family goes way back in Crescent Cove history. They've owned the newspaper and several other businesses for ages. They lived in Manhattan for most of Lane's life, but his mother finally got tired of the city life and they moved back here a few months ago. His dad commutes."

Grandmother smiled at Eliza. "Yes, I do recall hearing that now. I'll bet you didn't know that Lane's grandfather used to be a sweetheart of mine." She laughed. "Oh, it didn't last long, but I must say the poor boy was smitten."

"That's so amazing." Eliza smiled happily at Grandmother. "And it's his grandparents' house that Lane will be staying in!" She seemed to have renewed enthusiasm, like she knew she was suddenly back in Grandmother's good graces again.

"Oh, perhaps we can all get together sometime," gushed Grandmother.

Eliza nodded like this was a real possibility. "I'll be sure to let Lane know so he can tell his grandfather."

DJ wanted to point out that Lane's grandparents were supposedly on some cruise, but decided not to bother. Maybe some people were just better off with their heads in the sand. Like that old saying went — perhaps ignorance really was bliss.

"Well, I know you all have much to do. I've arranged for a town car to pick us up at noon. Hopefully we can do curbside check-in and get through security without too much delay. Our flight leaves at three fifty and we'll arrive in Fort Lauderdale around nine. From there it's about an hour's drive to Palm Beach. So it's going to be a long day. Hopefully you're all packed and just about ready to go."

"I need to finish packing," Eliza said suddenly.

"I need to start," said Casey.

"You haven't even started packing yet?" Grandmother looked disappointed. "What on earth are you—"

"I'll help her," offered Eliza. She smiled at Casey. "I'm an expert at packing. Just let me finish up and I'll come to your room and we'll have you ready in no time."

"Thank you, Eliza," said Grandmother. "I'm sure we'll all appreciate that."

DJ had to control herself in order not to roll her eyes at this show of gratitude. Seriously, her grandmother had the memory of a gnat.

10

spring breakdown

"Looks like Casey is Eliza's new best friend," DJ whispered to Taylor after observing Eliza sweetly begging the flight attendant for a seat change so the two girls could sit together.

"Or protégé," added Taylor. "Did you notice anything about Casey's traveling outfit?"

DJ studied Casey's pale blue velour jogging suit, which actually looked nothing like anything that Casey owned. "You mean that it belongs to Eliza?"

"Or that they look like twins." Taylor chuckled.

Eliza was wearing a pale gray jogging suit that was similar. Not only that, but both girls had on very similar oversized sunglasses as well as rhinestone-encrusted flip-flops.

"What is up with Casey?" DJ wondered aloud. "This is so not like her."

"She's either trying to make Eliza happy or she's lost her mind." Taylor nodded toward the two girls as they perused through the magazines they'd gotten at the air terminal newsstand. "Can you believe that Eliza's even got Casey reading *Vogue*? Casey hates *Vogue*."

"The next thing you know, Casey will be buttering up my grandmother and begging to be America's next top model."

Taylor laughed loudly.

"But at least Casey is okay," DJ said quietly. "I was actually pretty worried about her when she was missing this morning."

"Let's hope she's okay." Taylor frowned.

"What do you mean?"

"I mean she's not exactly herself today."

"Duh." DJ chuckled. "She's Eliza's clone."

DJ felt a tiny bit guilty when she looked up to where Rhiannon was sitting next to Grandmother. Rhiannon had gotten stuck being her companion. But to DJ's surprise, Rhiannon seemed perfectly happy. And the two of them were talking. Really talking. Probably about fads or style or design school or some other element of fashion that didn't particularly interest DJ. What interested DJ most at the moment was a nice long nap, and as soon as the jet took off she closed her eyes and leaned back.

When she woke up it was to the sound of a male voice. "So is Fort Lauderdale your final destination?" DJ opened her eyes to see a good-looking blond guy standing in the aisle and looking at Taylor with interest.

"Not exactly," Taylor's voice was coy, like she was playing her old cat-and-mouse game again. DJ sat up straighter and silently prayed this was not the case. *Please, don't go there, Taylor. Not again.*

"So you're not going down there for spring break?" he persisted with a hopeful smile.

"Yes, we're on spring break. But not in Fort Lauderdale."

"Too bad." He looked genuinely disappointed. "There's a lot going on down there."

"So I've heard." Her tone grew bored now, like she was losing interest. DJ felt relieved.

"So are you flying on to someplace else?" he asked. "Someplace more exciting and exotic? The Keys perhaps?"

"Not the Keys." Taylor sighed. "But where we're going is very nice."

"Sweet." He nodded eagerly then frowned. "But you're not going to tell me where it is, are you?"

"Just that it's supposed to be really beautiful."

Now he smiled at DJ. "Your friend's making this difficult," he told her. "Being very evasive about your final destination."

"And why shouldn't she be?" DJ smiled back. "After all, you're a stranger."

He laughed. "Oh yeah, stranger-danger. Now I remember what they told me in kindergarten. So let me introduce myself." He stuck out his hand to Taylor. "I'm Jeremy. And you?"

"Taylor." She nodded to DJ. "And this is Desiree."

"Desiree," he repeated as DJ jabbed Taylor with her elbow. "So now that we're not strangers, can I buy you girls a drink?" He glanced down the aisle to where the beverage cart was approaching them at the pace of an unmotivated slug.

Taylor grinned like she was enjoying this game again. "Thanks anyway, Jeremy, but the only kind of drinks we're drinking are free."

He looked seriously disappointed now. "That doesn't sound like much fun. I thought you said you were on spring break."

"We are." Taylor glanced over at DJ and winked. Then she turned back to the guy. "And you might be interested to know that we're taking a break from *high school*."

He looked surprised. "No way! I thought you were in college for sure."

"And you were wrong."

"You're pulling my leg, aren't you?"

"No. If you don't believe me, you can ask that woman with the silver hair sitting just a few rows ahead of us." Taylor pointed to Grandmother. "She's our chaperone."

"And my grandmother," DJ added. "And she'll be with us for the whole week."

He looked uncomfortable now. "Well, have fun in—whatever secret location you're headed to." He moved a few steps away from them, but paused next to where Eliza and Casey were sitting. And without even blinking an eye, he delivered the exact same line to them.

"Can you believe that guy?" DJ just shook her head.

"It's like he's trying to line up some action before he even gets off the plane," Taylor added. "Doesn't want to waste a minute."

"Although Eliza and Casey seem to be enjoying the attention," observed DJ.

"Hopefully they'll have the good sense to refuse the soon-to-be-offered drink."

DJ laughed. "After last night and with Grandmother just a few feet away, I should think so!"

The girls all seemed to wake up once they were in the limo and on their way to Palm Beach.

"I can't believe how warm it is here," said Rhiannon. "And it's almost ten o'clock."

"I can't wait to hit the beach tomorrow," said DJ. "I wonder if they rent surfboards anywhere near the general's house."

Grandmother laughed. "Yes, I'm sure all the retirees do a lot of surfing in Palm Beach."

"Not everyone there is old," Eliza informed them.

"How do you know?"

"Lane told me."

"How will we get around once we're at the general's house?" asked DJ. "Or is everything within walking distance?"

"The general keeps a car there," Grandmother informed them. "As well as a couple of bikes. Other than that, you'll have to use your legs or public transportation."

"Or cabs," suggested Eliza.

"And the rules will be similar to the ones in New York," Grandmother reminded them. "No girls out by themselves. You must stick to the buddy system. And you must let others know where you're going."

"What if you're not around?" asked Casey.

"We all have phones." Grandmother's voice grew stern. "And you can always leave notes in the house if necessary. But I will not have you girls running about willy-nilly with no one knowing where you are."

"When's the photo shoot?" asked Taylor.

"That's a very good question and I was just about to tell you. Josie has it all set for Tuesday. She'll send a car to pick us up at eight."

"Eight in the morning?" Eliza asked. "I thought this was a vacation."

"It's a working vacation. And don't forget you all agreed to this beforehand. No complaining if it turns out to be a long day, girls. And no staying up late the night before. You'll be photographed in the sun and, trust me, the camera will pick up everything. And that reminds me, you girls all be sure to use your sunscreen. Josie doesn't want to see anyone showing up looking like a lobster." She turned and stared at DJ. "And you know who I mean."

"But won't we need to get a little sun so that we look good in the swimwear shots?" asked Casey.

"A little sun is fine, as long as you're careful and use sunscreen. I just happen to know my granddaughter and she tends to forget. In fact, Taylor, I'd like to put you in charge of DJ's sunscreen, if you wouldn't mind."

Casey laughed. "That seems a little ridiculous, don't you think?"

"Why?" asked Taylor.

"Because ... well ... " Casey got uncomfortable. "You are, you know, naturally tan. Why should you be in charge of DJ's sunscreen?"

"It might interest you to know that women of color are advised to use sunscreen too."

"Really?" Casey looked doubtful.

"To prevent skin cancer."

"And I can attest to the fact that Taylor takes very good care of her skin." DJ looked at Taylor's gorgeous bronze skin and tried not to feel envy.

"As she should," said Grandmother. "As you all should."

Now Eliza whispered something to Casey and they both began to giggle. DJ wanted to tell them to "share it with the class," but knew that sounded just as juvenile as they were being and decided not to.

Finally, the driver turned into a gated community where Grandmother slipped in a key card and, presto, they were in. "This is really beautiful," said DJ as she admired the tall palm trees alongside a long pond with fountains. Everything was well illuminated with spotlights, and it really did look like paradise.

Before long they were unpacking their bags and going into a very elegant and spacious home.

"The general really is rich, isn't he?" Rhiannon said to Grandmother as she turned on a light in the great room.

Grandmother just nodded and smiled. "This is a lovely home."

"He'd be a pretty good catch," Rhiannon said quietly.

DJ tried to listen to her grandmother's response, but the other girls were making too much noise. Even so, she could tell by Grandmother's expression that this very idea may have been occurring to her as well. Certainly, she could do worse. Still, DJ wondered where she would fit into that picture. Not that it mattered terribly since she'd be in college next year anyway. But it did feel good to think she'd always have Carter House to come home to. Not that she planned to think about that now.

"I put dibs on our room," Taylor told DJ. "It opens right out to the pool."

DJ hadn't agreed to room with Taylor, but saw no reason to decline the invitation. "Cool," she said as she walked in. "I can roll out of bed and into the pool to do laps."

"Always our little athlete," said Eliza in a demeaning way.

"I want to stay in shape for soccer." DJ pointed to Casey now. "You might want to keep that in mind too. Don't forget we have playoffs when we get home."

"Ugh, don't remind me." Casey made a face.

"What do you mean?"

Casey pressed her lips together then looked over at Eliza. "Maybe I'll just quit it anyway."

"Seriously?" DJ stared at Casey. "Why?"

"Why not?" asked Eliza. "Girls aren't supposed to sweat like hogs."

DJ just rolled her eyes. "Yeah, whatever."

"I guess I'll get a room to myself," said Rhiannon.

"You can share with us," offered DJ. "That is, if you don't mind sharing a bed."

Rhiannon seemed to think about it. "You know, I think having a room to myself might be kind of nice for a change."

Taylor chuckled. "I think someone needs a break from her roommate."

Fortunately Eliza didn't hear this comment. She and Casey were already in their room with the door closed.

DJ got an idea. "Hey, Rhiannon, as well as those two seem to be getting along, you and Casey could probably switch rooms when we get back. Then you could be with Kriti."

"Wouldn't that be a nice break." Rhiannon smiled, then went into her room and closed the door.

Suddenly DJ began peeling off her clothes.

"Are you going to bed too?" asked Taylor in disappointment.

"No way." DJ nodded toward the pool as she unfastened her bra. "I'm going for a moonlight swim."

"I know," said Taylor in her old devilish tone. "Let's go skinny dipping."

DJ giggled. "Seriously?"

"It would be fun. We'll keep the lights off and we won't tell the others."

"What if the neighbors are looking?" DJ looked out to where the backs of some other houses faced the shared pool.

"All the lights are out," Taylor said as she pulled off her shirt. "Remember the old folks turn in early."

DJ giggled. "We'll have to be really quiet."

"Of course."

They both wrapped themselves in towels and tiptoed out their bedroom door, quietly creeping up to the pool. DJ looked carefully around to make sure no one was looking. Then they both peeled off their towels, dropped them next to the pool, and slid in. DJ couldn't help but giggle.

"Quiet," Taylor shushed her.

"Oh, wow," said DJ as she swam a silent stroke. "This water feels wonderful."

"It's like swimming in satin," whispered Taylor.

DJ dove under and swam half the length of the pool then quietly came up. The lights were dim, but she thought she could see ripples in the water where Taylor was on the other end. DJ went under again, silently swimming below the surface to the other end of the pool, and suddenly the lights went on!

DJ's heart was pounding as she clung to the side of the pool with only the top of her head above the water and frantically hoping that whatever had triggered the lights—if human—was not looking her way. She could hear footsteps and suddenly wondered if it might be Eliza and Casey, thinking they were very funny. But when she cautiously turned her head, she realized it was a man. And he had on a uniform and was carrying a night club.

"Nice night for a swim, pretty lady," he said to DJ.

"Can you turn those lights off?" she begged him. "Please."

"Did you forget your bathing suit?" he asked with a chuckle.

"As a matter of fact, I did." She was trying to see across the pool to where Taylor was—or had been—but the lights were so bright she felt blinded.

"I think you should get out," he told her.

"Not until you turn out those lights," she snapped back.

"Now don't make me get rough with you, pretty lady," he said in a creepy way. "But we have rules around here. For one thing, this is a members-only pool. For another thing, there's no swimming after ten at night. And besides that you're required to wear a swimsuit. I could have the police here in minutes."

"You don't need to call the police," DJ pleaded. "I'm a guest of General Harding."

"I'll just bet you are." The man laughed in an evil way, and DJ tried to see if Taylor was anywhere in sight.

"And I didn't know about the ten o'clock rule."

"But you figured this was a nudist colony, right?" He walked closer to her and actually extended his hand like he planned to help her out of the pool. "Come on, pretty lady, you cooperate and I won't call the cops."

"Stop right there," Taylor called from across the pool. Somehow, she had slipped out of the water and gotten her towel around her. She was now marching toward them with DJ's towel in hand.

"Oh, I see … there are two of you. Two pretty ladies."

"That's right." Taylor walked up and looked him right in the eyes, which wasn't difficult because she was as tall as he was. "And we are both guests of General Harding and my friend's grandmother, and our guardian is in the house right now. So if you want to press charges, I suggest you go over there and inform her first."

"Well, I might just do that."

"Fine," snapped Taylor. "In the meantime, I suggest you turn your back or we will have charges pressed against you. For your information we are both minors and we just arrived and haven't had a chance to learn about your rules. But we are guests here, not to mention good friends of the general's. If he hears how you've treated us, I'm sure you'll be looking for a new job in the morning."

Her words must have put the fear of something into him because he did turn around. And while he did, Taylor reached down and, using the towel as a shield, helped DJ out of the pool. DJ quickly wrapped her towel like a full-body sarong and they both marched past the guard.

"We're very sorry about breaking the rules," DJ called over her shoulder. "It won't happen again."

"And we'll be sure to let the general know you were doing your job," Taylor turned as she said this, "along with all the details."

DJ thought she saw the color draining from the man's face as he skulked away and within a minute the lights were turned off. "What a loser," said DJ angrily. "I hate to think of what he might've done if I'd been alone."

"Welcome to Palm Beach," said Taylor.

"Hopefully all the security guards aren't dirty old men," said DJ as they went into their room and locked the door and closed the drapes.

"I do intend to tell someone about that guy," Taylor said as she dropped her towel. "I'll bet he has a previous record as a sex offender."

"And even if the homeowners here are old, they deserve a decent security guard," added DJ.

"Don't kid yourself," said Taylor. "Guys like that might not care if a person was old or not."

DJ made a face. "Gross! That is just sick."

"Seems your grandmother was right," Taylor called from the bathroom.

"Huh?"

"Thank God for the buddy system."

DJ nodded as she sank down into a chair. "Thank God!" And she felt almost as thankful for Taylor just then—for her quick thinking and fast action. And later she would tell her.

11

spring breakdown

"Just so you know," DJ told the others the next morning. "The night security guard is a total perv."

"What?" demanded Grandmother as she poured her coffee.

"A pervert," DJ explained. "A degenerate."

"What are you talking about?"

The kitchen was quiet now and the others were listening too.

"DJ and I went for a little moonlight swim," Taylor explained as she poured some orange juice. "But we didn't know the pool was supposed to be closed, and suddenly the lights go on and this slimy little security guard is trying to pull DJ out of the pool and actually coming on to her like if she cooperated he wasn't going to call the police."

"He thought I was alone," DJ explained. And then she told about how Taylor came to her rescue.

"But the guy's a real lowlife," said Taylor. "And I think we should tell someone."

"We most certainly will," declared Grandmother. "I will call the general and ask him to see that this pervert person is relieved of his duties." She shook her finger at DJ now. "But no more after-hours swims, understand?"

"Trust me, I have no intention of doing that again."

"Still, that doesn't give anyone the right to take advantage." Grandmother had her phone out now. "I'm sure the general will be very concerned." She smiled now. "And I want to thank him for having his housekeeper stock the fridge for us."

"It figures the perv would go after DJ," teased Eliza after Grandmother left the room to converse with the general. "She's got that kind of appeal."

"What a horrid thing to say," Rhiannon shot back at her.

"I'm just kidding." Eliza made a face. "Can't anyone take a joke?"

Casey laughed. "I think it's funny."

"You would," said DJ with a scowl.

"And what's that supposed to mean?" Casey glared at DJ.

"Just that you used to think for yourself."

Casey rolled her eyes. "That shows how much you know." Then she walked away. But as she walked, DJ realized that she was, once again, dressed like Eliza. Probably wearing Eliza's clothes. When Eliza packed Casey's bags, she likely threw out all of Casey's oddball garments, replacing them with expensive designer clothes that Eliza wouldn't be embarrassed to be seen with. Poor Casey.

"Why is everything such a competition with some people?" Rhiannon was putting a layer of cream cheese on her bagel. Only Taylor and DJ were with her in the kitchen now.

Taylor laughed. "Not that you're mentioning names."

"It just gets so tiring. I mean, it's so junior high, don't you think?"

Now Taylor looked slightly hurt. "You mean me, don't you?"

Rhiannon blinked in surprise. "No."

"I know I'm competitive," Taylor admitted. "It's probably one of my worst faults."

"Honestly, I didn't mean you." Rhiannon looked directly at Taylor.

"Me then?" asked DJ, suddenly feeling slightly guilty.

"No. I didn't mean you either."

"But I'm pretty competitive too."

"Only when it comes to sports." Taylor laughed. "The rest of the time you're a pushover."

"I'm a pushover?" DJ felt offended.

"I meant that in the best possible way. You're easy to get along with," Taylor persisted. "Why else would I want you for my roommate? I'm the one who's difficult. And I'm too competitive too." She looked at Rhiannon again. "You did mean me, didn't you?"

"You guys had to know that I meant Eliza." Rhiannon jabbed her cream cheese spreader in the air like a sword. "It's like she just never quits. She never gives up. Even this whole thing with Casey is feeling like a great big ridiculous competition. It's like Eliza lost Kriti so she wanted to carve me into her new best friend, and I played along for a while—just to be nice. But then I drew the line and refused. And so she went after Casey. And now she keeps throwing poor Casey in my face—like *so there*! Or so it seems." Rhiannon sighed and took a bite of her bagel.

"You're probably right," agreed DJ.

"And Casey is a big girl," Taylor pointed out. "She'll probably get tired of Eliza's game before long. And she'll possibly learn a good lesson from all this."

"In the meantime, she's eating it up," said DJ.

Taylor shrugged. "I'm sure we've all been there and done that in one form or another."

They joined the others in the living room now. Grandmother had finished informing the general about the creepy security guard and Eliza was begging to borrow the general's car.

"Where do you want to go?" Grandmother asked.

"Shopping," Eliza announced like it was a good thing.

"Why?" demanded DJ. "Didn't you shop your brains out before we got here?"

"Yes, but that was before I shared my wardrobe with someone in need." Eliza gave DJ a placating look. "Now I realize I'll be running short. And Casey needs a few things too, don't you, Case?"

Casey just looked down at her feet, which were wearing Eliza's sandals.

"And we want to get our shopping done before the boys arrive."

"Which will be when?" inquired Grandmother.

"Around six."

"Perhaps we should invite them for dinner," suggested Grandmother.

"Oh, could we?" Eliza asked with enthusiasm. "I'd be happy to pay for the food."

Grandmother smiled. "I think that would be lovely. I noticed a basket in the kitchen that's just full of brochures from local restaurants and caterers. Why don't you see what you can put together, Eliza?"

"Just make sure there's no booze this time," DJ said loudly.

"That's right!" Grandmother shook her fist in the air. "No alcohol!"

"Now who wants to go surfing with me today?" DJ called out. "I found a surf shop in the yellow pages and it's within walking distance." She looked hopefully at Taylor.

"I used to surf," Taylor told her. "Back when I was young and crazy and didn't care if I ended up looking like a drowned rat with bad hair and broken nails."

DJ moaned. "There's more to life than looking good."

Taylor nodded. "I know, but life's more fun when you do."

DJ looked at Casey. "There was a time when you'd have gone with me . . . but I'm guessing that's not today."

Casey smiled and shrugged. "Sorry, DJ, I already have plans."

"Rhiannon?" DJ made a begging gesture with her hands.

"You know I'm scared of water, DJ. I'm a horrible swimmer."

"Right." She looked at Grandmother then shook her head. "You guys are all a bunch of old ladies!" Then she went to her room, hoping that someone would feel sorry for her. Unfortunately it didn't work.

"I'm sorry, DJ," said Taylor when she finally came to check on her. "I'm just not into surfing."

"I got that."

"But . . . " Taylor grinned. "If we found a game of beach volleyball, I might be willing to get a little sweaty."

"All right!"

"As long as I get some down time too. I was really looking forward to just vegging on the beach."

"Absolutely."

"Should we see if Rhiannon wants to come?"

And so the three of them set off for the beach. Thankfully, Rhiannon and Taylor both remembered their sunscreen and they made sure that DJ had plenty. And before long, they did find a volleyball game. Taylor, true to her word, played good and hard. Rhiannon made an attempt, but she just wasn't the athletic type, and before long everyone was glad to see her move to the sidelines.

"This reminds me of when we first met," Taylor told DJ during a break. "Remember being at the beach last summer?"

DJ laughed. "I remember the bag mix up."

Taylor snickered. "And you thought the condoms were candy."

DJ groaned. "Please, don't remind me. That could still go on record as one of my most embarrassing moments."

"You seem to get more than your fair share."

"And now I can add last night to the list."

Rhiannon came over to join them. "Are you guys hungry yet?"

They decided to tell their volleyball friends good-bye and go off in search of food. "I'm thinking rock shrimp," Taylor told them. "I've heard they're really good around here."

"I was thinking something cheap like a hotdog," admitted Rhiannon.

"What if it's my treat?" offered Taylor.

"Bring it!" said Rhiannon happily.

Before long, Taylor had discovered an outdoor café that boasted the best rock shrimp in Palm Beach.

"I don't know if this is the best or not," DJ declared as she finished her lunch. "But it's the best I've ever had."

"Yeah, thanks!" Rhiannon actually licked her finger, and then she pointed out toward the walkway. "Look at that!"

They all turned to see.

"Is that Eliza and Casey?" DJ removed her sunglasses and squinted in the sunlight. "I mean, it looks like them, except that they're ... like ... *orange?*"

Taylor broke into laughter. "I bet they went to a spray-on-tan booth."

"A really bad spray-on-tan booth," said DJ.

"What about the photo shoot?" Rhiannon sounded worried.

"Maybe it'll wear off by then," said DJ.

Taylor stood and waved at the two girls, calling them over to their sidewalk table. "Hey, did you guys have lunch yet?" Taylor looked like she was about to lose it.

"It looks like they had oranges for lunch," said DJ.

"Very funny." Eliza glared at them.

"No, we haven't had lunch." Casey looked like she wanted to hit somebody. "We went shopping and ... well, other things."

"Obviously," said DJ. "Anyway, we can recommend the rock shrimp here." She held out one last one in case they were interested. "In fact, it kind of matches your skin."

"I was thinking more along the line of Cheetos," teased Taylor. "Seriously, have you guys looked in the mirror lately?"

Eliza narrowed her eyes. "Yes, but thanks for reminding us. I've already put my lawyer onto it. A certain day spa is going to be served shortly."

"What happened?" asked Rhiannon.

"It was her idea." Casey jerked her thumb toward Eliza.

"I've had lots of spray-on tans." Eliza shrugged. "It's never been a big deal."

"Until now." DJ just shook her head.

"But HOW did it happen?" persisted Rhiannon. "How did you both end up looking like tangerines?"

"This idiot girl claimed she knew what she was doing." Casey rolled her eyes. "She looked like she was about twelve and she was running the tanning section. She happily agreed to let us both get sprayed at the same time—too bad I didn't wait to see how Eliza looked first."

"So we picked the color we wanted—Malibu Gold," Eliza continued. "And this devil child punched the supposed formula into the computer. Then we went into the booths and got sprayed."

"What will you do about the photo shoot?" asked the ever practical Rhiannon.

"We're working on it." Eliza grimaced as she held up a glitzy pink bag. "These products are supposed to help."

"Are you still planning on having the guys for dinner tonight?"

"I already ordered the food and called Lane," Eliza said quickly. "But I'm thinking of canceling."

To her surprise, DJ actually felt sorry for the two orange girls. "Maybe we can help put things together for you tonight," she said suddenly.

"While you two are exfoliating," added Taylor.

"Do you think it would help to soak in the pool?" offered Rhiannon. "I mean, before you exfoliate or whatever it is you're going to do?"

"What about the ocean?" suggested DJ. She wanted to add "so you don't leave an orange ring around the pool," but thought better or if. "Maybe the wave action and salt water can help remove the dye—kind of like a washing machine."

"Maybe." Eliza nodded. "That's not a bad idea."

"Anyway, we'll do whatever we can to help," Rhiannon assured them.

"Thanks." Now Eliza almost smiled.

"Yeah, thanks." Casey actually seemed grateful.

"I'm sure it'll come off," DJ called out as the two walked away.

"I hope you're right," said Taylor. "That could really mess up the photo shoot."

"What if Josie makes us pay her back for the airfare and everything?" Rhiannon looked seriously worried now. "I mean, I've saved up some money for school, but that would wipe it out."

"We'll figure out something," Taylor said with confidence. "One way or another, we'll get those girls looking photoworthy by Tuesday. If nothing else, we could get some bronzer and their skin could be as dark as mine."

"And Rhiannon and I will look like albinos next to you guys," said DJ.

"And now that we offered to help with dinner, I insist we get some down time before it's time for KP," said Taylor. "I'm heading back to the house."

No one argued. But once they were back, DJ felt restless, and since it was daylight and the pool was open, she decided to swim laps. After that, she fell asleep in the sun and when she woke up, she realized she'd forgotten the sunscreen. Still, it wasn't like she was seriously burnt. Just a little pink.

Of course, that pink got brighter as evening came. And when Grandmother saw DJ arranging things on the patio table, she let out a little cry.

DJ nearly dropped the stack of plates. "What's wrong?"

"Oh, Desiree, I thought I told you to use sunscreen!"

"And I thought you'd agreed to call me DJ, Grandmother. Remember?"

Grandmother pressed her forefinger onto DJ's arm, releasing it to expose a white spot. "You are burnt to a crisp, child!"

"It'll turn into a tan in a day or two," DJ assured her. "It always does."

"And I already lathered her up in a special Aloe Vera after-sun product," Taylor said as she set some glasses on the table. "I promise you, she'll look great by Tuesday."

"I certainly hope so. It's bad enough that we've come here one girl short. But if we show up with DJ looking like a cooked crab, we could be in trouble."

"Speaking of seafood, Mrs. Carter . . . " Taylor glanced at DJ. "You haven't seen Eliza and Casey, have you?"

Grandmother frowned. "I was just about to ask why you girls were getting things ready for dinner. I thought Eliza was seeing to it."

"We're helping," DJ said quickly.

"And what time is dinner?" Grandmother asked.

"Eliza said the guys should be here by seven thirty."

"Seems she should be here then." Grandmother pointed to the oversized clock. "It's past seven now. Where is that girl?"

"Actually, I think Eliza and Casey *are* here," Rhiannon said cautiously.

"Really?" Grandmother looked perplexed. "Then where are they?"

"I just heard them going into their room. I, uh, I think they're getting ready."

"Well, I have the utmost respect for primping and looking one's best, but those girls should be in here helping too." Grandmother strode off toward the direction of their room on the other side of the house.

"Oh no," said Rhiannon. "I guess I should've kept my mouth shut."

"She's going to see them anyway," DJ pointed out.

"And maybe they're—" Taylor's voice was drowned out by the sound of Grandmother's high-pitched scream.

"Do you think I should call 911?" asked DJ. She was only partly kidding.

"Let's go make sure she hasn't had a stroke."

All three of them raced toward Eliza and Casey's room. And there, supporting herself with both hands in the open doorway with her jaw hanging down, stood Grandmother. And in front of her were the two orange girls in their bikinis. In fact, they seemed even oranger now than they'd been previously.

Eliza was talking fast, explaining the day spa, the spray paint, the wrong formula, and how they were going to be sued by the Wiltons' attorney.

"They should be sued," agreed Grandmother, "but that doesn't help us now."

"We have some product here." Eliza held up a bottle. "But we thought it would help to swim in the ocean first, so that's where we've been."

"Yes," Casey said quickly. "DJ suggested it and it seemed to make sense."

"Salt water?" Grandmother rubbed her chin. "Yes, as I recall salt water was good for … *good for setting dye!*"

"Setting dye?"

Grandmother turned to DJ now. "Did you tell them that on purpose?"

"So the dye would be set?" DJ shook her head. "No, of course not! I just thought tumbling around in the ocean would help to wear it off. My swimsuits always seem to fade after being in the ocean — or maybe it's the pool."

"Well, I remember when I was a little girl and if my mother dyed something, like cloth or Easter eggs, she seemed to add salt to set it."

"Fantastic." Eliza drew in a sharp breath and made a fist.

Both Eliza and Casey were glaring at DJ now. "Honestly," she told them. "I had no idea. I mean, I don't even take chemistry. And it just seemed like—"

"Get out of here!" screamed Eliza.

"Well!" Grandmother stepped back.

"I don't mean you, Mrs. Carter." Eliza spoke between her teeth. "But your granddaughter is not welcome!"

DJ backed away just as Eliza slammed the door. Grandmother remained in the room and seemed to be trying to console the girls, not that it was helping.

"Suddenly this is my fault?" DJ peered at Taylor and Rhiannon. "Now I'm the bad guy just because I suggested a dip in the ocean might help?"

"Who knows?" said Taylor. "They might've turned green if they'd gone into the pool."

"Don't take it personally, DJ." Rhiannon patted her gently on the back. "They're the ones who got sprayed orange."

"I know." But even as she said this, she did feel a little responsible. For a brief moment it had seemed like all five of them were starting to get along, like maybe this was actually going to be a fun week. Oh, why hadn't she just kept her big mouth shut?

12

spring breakdown

Eliza and Casey came to dinner wearing long sleeves and long pants and heavy foundation. The guys had already arrived and everyone was out on the patio, with some already eating while others were filling their plates at the buffet table that Taylor, DJ, and Rhiannon had arranged.

"About time the hostess arrived," teased Lane as Eliza stepped onto the patio. "I thought you were the one who invited me to dinner and you don't even show up."

"Sorry, Casey and I had some — uh — "

"This Greek food is killer, Eliza," said Taylor quickly. "What a great restaurant find."

"Yeah," agreed DJ. "You and Casey better get some of that grape leaf salad stuff before it disappears." She shoved plates at the two girls. "We purposely kept the lights dim out here," she whispered to them. "You both look almost natural."

"Thanks a lot," Eliza hissed quietly.

"By the way," DJ said, "I did some quick research on the general's computer and salt does NOT set dye."

"Set dye?" Lane had obviously been trying to eavesdrop.

"We were talking about tie-dye," Taylor said quickly.

"And salt doesn't help it much," added DJ.

"Oh, I'm so relieved," said Eliza sarcastically.

Lane laughed. "You girls are so funny."

"Speaking of funny, there's that nasty security guard," Taylor said quietly as she nodded toward the pool. "I thought maybe he'd be fired by now."

"Ho-ho ... a nasty security guard?" Harry's brows lifted with interest as he glanced over to the pool area. "What does he do that's so nasty?"

So, to distract the others from Eliza and Casey's situation, DJ launched into the story of how she and Taylor got caught using the pool after hours.

"And then the perv tries to pull DJ out of the pool," Taylor added.

"What's so perverted about that?" asked Lane.

Taylor laughed and looked around as if trying to see who was listening then she lowered her voice. "Just the fact that we were skinny dipping."

DJ looked to see if Grandmother was within earshot. Thankfully, she'd gone back into the house.

"Skinny dipping?" cried Eliza. "You never told us that part of the story."

"And don't go and tell Mrs. Carter either," Taylor warned her. "Because when it comes to telling secrets, we've got plenty of dirt on you, girlfriend."

Eliza laughed. "Why would I tell Mrs. Carter?" She turned to DJ now. "I cannot believe Miss Goody-Two-Shoes went skinny dipping."

Lane nudged Harry and grinned. "Looks like we guys came a day late."

DJ knew her face was red, but hoped it just blended with her sunburn. Still, she wanted to change to a more comfortable subject. "Hey, are any of you guys into surfing?" she said loudly. "Because I can't get any of these girlie girls to hang ten with me."

"You're a surfer?" Lane's eyes lit up. "No way!"

"Hey, I grew up in Southern California," she tossed back. "It's been awhile, but I think I can remember how to do it."

"Is there a rental shop around?"

"Less than a mile from here."

"I'm in," he said. "How about tomorrow?"

"Works for me." She turned to the other guys now. "Any other surfer dudes wanna come?"

"I'd give it a try," said Seth. "It's probably kind of like snowboarding, right?"

"Absolutely," said DJ. "Only wetter." She looked at Casey now. "You used to surf, Case. How about—"

"I don't think so," Casey said in an icy tone.

Then DJ remembered the dye job. Still, was Casey going to let that ruin her fun?

"I'd like to try surfing," said Bradford. He glanced at Rhiannon. "How about you?"

She gave him a half smile. "Remember, I can't even swim very well."

"You should learn," DJ told her. "Maybe I can give you lessons in the pool while we're here."

Rhiannon actually looked interested. "Yeah, maybe ... "

"Why wait for lessons?" said Bradford as he grabbed Rhiannon and picked her up, carrying her over to the pool like he was going to dump her.

Rhiannon started to squeal and DJ ran over to help. "You're not really going to drop her, are you?" she asked Bradford. The next thing she knew, someone had his arms around her. She turned to see it was Lane. And suddenly all the guys were grabbing girls and within minutes everyone was in the pool. DJ didn't really mind since she had her swimsuit on beneath her shorts anyway. But Eliza and Casey were furious.

"Thanks a lot!" Eliza snarled at Lane as she pulled her soggy self out of the pool. But her velour warm-up pants were so soaked that they'd slipped down to expose a big patch of orange skin.

"Hey," said Lane. "You're turning orange, Eliza."

"So is Casey," called out Bradford. "What's up with you two?"

"They got into some bad tanning dye," DJ explained quickly.

"Thanks for telling the world," snapped Eliza. She turned and glared at DJ. But what she didn't know was that her makeup was now dripping down in stripes and looked hilarious.

"Hey, Tiger Woman," called out Lane. "You're looking mighty fierce."

"Their faces are striped," hooted Seth. "Is it Halloween?"

Both Casey and Eliza turned their backs and slosh-marched back toward the house while everyone else laughed loudly.

"Don't give them too bad of a time," DJ said between giggles. "They've had a hard day."

But as the rest of them sat around in damp clothes, continuing to eat and talk and laugh, Casey and Eliza didn't return. DJ suspected they were in their room pouting — or perhaps exfoliating. She never would've guessed they were drinking.

DJ had been so relieved to see the guys arriving at the party without alcohol, either on them or on their breath. It had almost given her hope. That is, until she went in to tell Eliza and Casey good night as well as to apologize and perhaps convince Casey to come surfing with them tomorrow.

"Don'tcha believe in knocking?" Eliza said to her in a slurred voice as she hid something in the bathroom.

"I did knock," DJ told her.

"We didn't hear you," Casey shot back at her.

"Then turn down the TV," DJ told her. She went closer to see what was in Casey's glass, but the smell was her tip off. "You guys are drinking!" she exclaimed.

Casey just shrugged.

"Do you not remember what my grandmother said?"

"Who cares?" Eliza shot back. "It's not like we're going to have any fun anyway. Just look at us." She stood in front of the closet mirror and looked like she was about to start crying again.

"I read online that spray-on tans should start to fade within a few days," DJ told her.

"In the meantime, I can be found right here," Eliza said sadly.

"Maybe this is your chance to see that life isn't just about how you look," DJ told her.

Eliza actually laughed. "Yeah, right!"

"Seriously," persisted DJ. "What if you got in an accident and suddenly lost your looks?"

"I have been in an accident," she protested. "A spraying accident."

"Do you know how many girls would happily trade their looks for yours, Eliza?" DJ stepped over and looked her square in the eyes. "Orange skin and all?"

Eliza just shrugged.

"You take it all for granted too," DJ continued. "But maybe this is your opportunity to think about the inner Eliza — look beyond your appearance for a change." Now DJ turned to Casey. "And what about you?"

"What about me?" Casey held up her glass to the light and studied it.

"You were never like this."

"Like what?"

"So into your looks."

"People change." She narrowed her eyes at DJ now. "Take you for instance, DJ. You've changed."

"How?"

"You used to be a loyal friend."

"Used to?"

"Yeah . . . then it's like you're only loyal to Taylor."

DJ didn't know what to say.

"And I know why," Casey continued. "It's because you're just as shallow as the rest of them. Taylor is beautiful and you like being with the beautiful people. Well, maybe that's what I'm doing too."

Eliza held up her hands hopelessly. "The beautiful ORANGE people."

"Maybe you should start a cult," said DJ in a flat voice. "The beautiful, orange, shallow people who allow their looks to dictate whether or not they can have a good time."

Casey held up her glass like she was toasting. "Hey, I'm having a good time."

"Yeah, right. It looks like you're having a pity party—a pity party of two." She shook her finger at Casey now. "And you love surfing, Case! But you're not going to just because you're so obsessed with your looks."

"Am not!" Casey stood up now, staggering slightly. "Take it back."

"I won't." DJ stepped away from her.

"I am not obshesh—obseshed—whatever you just said."

124

DJ laughed. "Okay, then prove it tomorrow. Come surfing with us."

"Fine." Casey shook an orange fist in the air. "I will!"

"Maybe I will too," said Eliza.

DJ blinked. "Seriously, you know how to surf?"

"No, I don't. But there's a first time for everything, right?"

DJ grinned. "Absolutely. And we'll be happy to help you learn." Then DJ went into the bathroom to see that Eliza had put a bottle of vodka on the counter. It was half full and DJ took the liberty of emptying the rest of it down the drain before she left.

13

spring breakdown

DJ wasn't that surprised when Eliza decided not to join the surfers the next day. But she was pleased that Casey remained true to her word.

"Look at you girls," said Grandmother in a tone that did not sound positive. All five girls were puttering around the kitchen, getting coffee or green tea or yogurt or toasting bagels, all in various stages of dress and mostly with bed-head hair. Not that DJ cared since she'd be surfing soon anyway.

"Yeah, look at us," said DJ as she stuck a spoon into her yogurt.

"I am serious," continued Grandmother. "All five of you line up there for a minute, please." She pointed to the breakfast bar. "Right there."

So they lined up and Grandmother stood frowning at them. "My girls. My lovely, lovely girls. Two orange. One red. One white and freckled. And one ... " She smiled at Taylor. "Thank goodness for you, dear!"

"So nice that you don't have favorites," said DJ as she moved away from the lineup.

Grandmother shook her finger at DJ now. "If you'd only have listened to me and not turned yourself into a lobster, you'd be my favorite too."

"Gee, thanks." DJ rolled her eyes. "So much for depth of character and not giving into superficiality or shallowness."

"The point is" — Grandmother ignored DJ's slam — "that Josie has paid our way here so that you girls can show off her new line of swimwear. But how is that possible now?" She sank down onto a chair in the breakfast nook and sighed. "I feel like an utter failure."

Taylor went over and placed a hand on Grandmother's shoulder now. "It'll be okay," she said gently. "I'm sure we can get it together by then."

Grandmother shook her head. "I don't see how."

"For one thing, DJ's burn will be a nice even tan by then."

"DJ!" Grandmother shook her fist. "You make sure you have on lots of sunscreen today. And make sure it's waterproof."

DJ saluted her. "Yes, sir. I mean, yes, ma'am."

"And worst-case scenario with Casey and Eliza is that we'll lather them in bronzer for the shoot. Josie should be pleased to have such tanned girls."

"And what about me?" Rhiannon asked sadly. "I'm the white and freckled one, remember."

"You are beautiful," DJ told her. "Just the way you are."

Grandmother nodded and sniffed. "DJ is right, Rhiannon. I shouldn't have said what I did. You'll be just fine. In fact, Josie wanted you girls to look natural."

"And we are," said DJ. "Well, except for our Orange Crush girls, but they'll be fine by then."

"Remember when Daisy and I had blue hair," Casey reminded Grandmother. "And that turned out okay."

Grandmother nodded. "Yes, I suppose you're right."

"So, don't worry so much," Taylor told her.

"All right." Grandmother stood and held her head high. "I will *not* worry. But I'm warning you girls, if any more of you come home looking weird or green or bald or maimed or anything that changes your appearances, I will not be held responsible for Josie's reaction on Tuesday."

DJ wondered how that was even possible since it was Grandmother who'd arranged this whole thing in the first place, but she certainly wasn't going to mention that now.

"I told the guys we'd meet them at the surf shop," DJ told Casey, "as soon as it opened, which is like now."

Casey looked down at her orange arms and legs and sighed. "This is not going to be easy."

"You don't have to go," Eliza told her. "I wouldn't if I were you."

"We know that already," DJ said quickly. "But you are not her, okay?"

"Even if you do look like the Orange Sisters," teased Taylor.

"See." Casey used this to make her point. "Everyone is going to laugh at me."

"Get over yourself," DJ told her. "Everyone laughs at everyone anyway. It's just how we're wired. Besides, if you can do this with a sense of humor, it will build character."

Casey laughed sarcastically.

"DJ is right," Rhiannon told her. "You should go, Casey. You'll probably be glad you did."

"Fine." Casey grabbed her bag. "Let's go!"

And Casey got teased some on the way to the surf shop and then by the guys who were there, but after awhile, she seemed to take it in stride. They even seemed to let up, and before long they were all out on their boards trying to catch a wave. And as DJ watched Casey finally getting up (after several nasty wipeouts) and having a nice ride, she felt pretty sure that Casey was no longer concerned about the color of her skin.

"You're not bad," Lane told DJ as they sat straddling their boards and waiting for another good wave.

"You're not bad yourself," she told, "I mean, for an East Coast boy."

"And you're not an East Coast girl?"

She thought about it. "Not really. I mean, my mom's family is East Coast, but growing up in California, I always considered myself as West Coast."

"Is that superior?"

She laughed. "Not according to people like you."

"Are you saying I'm a snob?"

She shrugged.

"You are?" He looked crushed. "Did you guys hear that?" he called to the others. "DJ thinks I'm a snob."

"You are a snob," called back Seth. "So is Bradford."

Bradford laughed. "Glad to know who my friends really are."

"DJ's right," Casey tossed out, "some of you East Coast boys are snobs. And so are some of the girls. People in California aren't like that."

"Yeah, right!" Lane laughed. "Can you hear yourself?"

So then they got into a who's better argument—East verses West—and almost didn't notice as a great wave came their way. It was big enough for all of them to ride and soon they were up. But just as quickly, Bradford and Seth went down and only Lane, DJ, and Casey were riding. Then Lane went down, and it was just DJ and Casey side by side. DJ reached over to attempt a high five and Casey slapped back, which sent them both tumbling. They emerged from the water laughing.

"I'm so glad you came today," DJ told Casey. "This feels like old times."

"California wins!" shouted Lane as he came over to join them. "And I say winners buy lunch."

"Ha!" DJ shot back at him. "Losers buy. After all, you're the rich, snooty East Coast snobs."

As it turned out, the guys did buy lunch. But since they all settled for hotdogs and smoothies, DJ knew it wasn't going to break their budgets. "Hey, Casey," she said pointing to her face, "the orange is starting to fade a little."

"Seriously?" Casey looked hopeful.

"Yeah." Lane studied her closely. "Now it's gone down from tangerine to more like ... maybe overripe cantaloupe."

"You cute little fruit, you," teased Seth.

"Hey, watch who you're calling a fruit," she fired back. And then they were wrestling on the sand.

"Puh-leeze," said DJ, "there are children watching."

"Get a room," teased Bradford.

DJ shifted on the sand so she didn't have to watch Casey and Seth making out. Seriously, why did they have to act like that? The old Casey would've made fun of someone for being such an exhibitionist. But, like Case had said just last night, people change. And so far whatever was going on between Casey and Seth was "nobody's business," or at least that's what Casey said if DJ asked. Casey had made it pretty clear that she wanted DJ to butt out of her personal life.

"Penny for your thoughts?" Lane asked her.

"My thoughts are worth more than a penny."

"Yeah, yeah, what with inflation, I'll give you a nickel."

She punched him in the arm. "They're worth way more than that."

He pulled out his waterproof billfold and opened it.

"Stop — stop!" she cried as he pulled out a small stack of bills. "Put that away before I get arrested for soliciting or something equally skanky."

He laughed and put his money away.

Bradford was on his cell phone now, apparently with Rhiannon, and it sounded like they were making plans to check out an art gallery that Bradford's mom was interested in.

"Are you going to do any more surfing?" Lane asked her.

"I'd like to." She glanced over to where Seth and Casey were still locking lips and rolled her eyes. "I'm not so sure about those two though."

Bradford closed his phone. "Rhiannon and I want to do some sightseeing, anyone else interested?"

"I want to keep surfing," Lane told him.

"How about you?" Bradford called out to Seth.

"I'm ready to hang it up." Seth sat up and brushed the sand off. "I think I've swallowed enough sea water for the day." He pulled Casey up by the hand. "How about you, Cheeto?"

"Funny." She shook the sand from her hair into his face.

"So ... " Bradford looked at Lane. "If you're going to stick around here to surf, do you mind if we take the car?"

Lane shrugged. "Not if DJ will let me hang at the girls' place until you pick me up."

"Sounds like a plan. I'll head back to the house to clean up first." Bradford looked at Seth now. "You coming?"

"Yeah." Seth grabbed Casey's hand, pulling her to her feet. "Me and my orange girl."

The three of them grabbed up their boards and stuff and suddenly it was just Lane and DJ.

"Ready to rock and roll?" Lane asked as he picked up his board.

"Oh, yeah!" DJ grinned at him. "I'll do the rocking and I'm guessing you'll be the one to roll."

"Ha-ha," he said sarcastically.

"Oh, wait." She grabbed her bag and fished around. "I need to put on sunscreen or my grandmother will kill me."

She started lathering up her arms and shoulders and legs and the next thing she knew, Lane was rubbing some onto her back.

"You don't want to miss anything," he warned as he massaged in the lotion. "You swimsuit models gotta look your best."

"Thanks a lot," she said as she grabbed back the sunscreen and shoved it into her bag.

"Hey, don't I get any? Or don't you care if I go home with third-degree burns?"

"Sorry." She tossed the bottle back to him, waiting as he covered his shoulders and chest and face. "That should do it, unless you want to get my back."

She gave him a look then grabbed back the lotion and squirted a big blob onto his back. Of course, it took a long time to rub it in.

"Ooh, that feels good," he said in a teasing tone. "Yeah, right there."

"That's enough." She slapped the middle of his back, grabbed up her board, and took off toward the water.

Soon they were out there again, straddling their boards and waiting for a good wave, but other than a couple of little sleepers, the action seemed to have died down.

"I could get used to this." Lane stretched his arms up toward the sky and sighed loudly. "Sun, sand, waves . . . I think I might like to become a beach bum when I grow up."

DJ laughed. "Such high aspirations. I'm sure your parents will be proud."

"Yeah, can you imagine their faces if I told them I was giving up Yale to be a surfer dude?"

"You're going to Yale?"

"Probably. Or that's what my old man thinks. I'm still waiting for acceptance."

"My grandmother made me apply to Yale." DJ laughed hard now. "Just because my great-grandfather and a few other smart family members went there. I only sent it in to make her happy, but it's so not going to happen."

"Why's that?"

"For one thing I'm not terribly academic. I mean, my grades are okay. But not anything like Kriti. Or even Taylor." DJ smacked the water. "That Taylor comes across so nonchalant and hardly even studies and yet she pulls out these stunning grades. I used to think she was sleeping with some of her teachers."

"Maybe she was."

DJ shook her head. "No. Flirting maybe, but that was all. Besides some of her teachers are women—"

"And—"

"And, please do not go there."

"Still, that doesn't explain why you couldn't get into Yale."

"You're nuts," she told him. "It's impossible."

"Not necessarily. And I can tell you why."

"Fine, knock yourself out."

"First of all, you're a great athlete and Yale can always get into that. Second of all, you have family connections. Third of all, you're well liked at school. I even heard you were homecoming queen."

"By write in." She laughed. "I think it was a joke. I mean, you should've seen me with my broken leg and—"

"Another thing. You're the hometown hero girl. And,"—he pointed his finger in the air—"you are a professional model! I rest my case."

"And—" She leaned over and began paddling. "Here comes our wave!"

"And," he called after her, "you're a darn good surfer."

She glanced over her shoulder just in time to see him wipe out. Then she continued to ride the wave, thinking of nothing else until the wave died down and she sank into the water. That was good.

Lane was still blowing water out of his nose when she rejoined him. "Man, you really bit into that wave, dude."

"Yeah, I think I drank about a gallon of water too."

"Are you okay?"

He nodded then shook his head like he had water in his ears.

"We can call it quits if you want," she offered. "I'd hate to take you back to Eliza half-drowned. She already hates me enough as it is."

"And what is up with that?"

"I wish I knew. A lot of girls are competitive, but Eliza takes it to a whole new level."

"And it usually backfires on her."

"You've noticed?"

He nodded.

"I just wish she could let her hair down." DJ sighed. "I mean, she might be fun to know if she could just relax." She turned to Lane. "And I mean *without* alcohol."

He nodded. "I know."

"Sorry, I didn't mean to dis on your girlfriend."

"That's the thing."

"What's the thing?"

"I don't want Eliza for my girlfriend."

DJ leaned back her head and stared up at the sky. "Please, do not say you're going to break up with her. At least not down here in Palm Beach."

"Why?"

She turned and looked at him. "Because Eliza will make us all even more miserable than she's already doing."

"So I have to pretend like I'm still into her? For a whole week?"

DJ nodded. "Yeah, that would be the kind thing to do."

He groaned.

Suddenly DJ got worried. "This doesn't have anything to do with me, does it? Because if it does, you can forget about—"

"No, DJ, Miss Center of the Universe, it doesn't have anything to do with you."

"Whew!" Then she turned and glared at him. "And I am not Miss Center of the Universe, thank you very much. I'm sure there are plenty of other girls far more worthy of that particular title."

He chuckled. "Yeah, I have to agree with you there. Take Eliza for instance ... please, take her!"

DJ shook her finger at him. "Not nice."

"Okay, DJ, for your sake I will try to keep Miss Eliza happy for the next few days, but I cannot promise anything."

"Thank you."

"Did you know that Eliza thinks shopping is a hobby?"

DJ laughed. "As a matter of fact, I did know that."

"I mean, she has no real interests."

"Well, there's fashion." DJ thought hard. "And ... " She thought even harder. "And there's ... "

"Shopping," he finished. "Seriously, that's it."

"Well, if shopping was an Olympic event, Eliza would be sure to win."

"Well, look what the cat dragged in," said Eliza as DJ appeared in the great room. "Did you have a good time with my boyfriend?"

DJ made a face at her. "As a matter of fact, I brought him home for you." She nodded over her shoulder to where Lane was slipping off his flip-flops.

Eliza sat up straighter. "Well, that was thoughtful of you, DJ. Guess I owe you one."

DJ forced a smile. "And if you'll excuse me, I'm going to clean up."

"Not that you need it," teased Eliza.

"Thanks."

"That whole seaweed in the hair thing is so becoming."

DJ was tempted to comment on Eliza's rusty complexion and thought better of it. No need to start a catfight.

DJ went into her room and found a note from Taylor saying that she and Harry probably wouldn't be back until after dinner. DJ stripped out of her damp things and then, relieved to have the room to herself, took her time showering and cleaning up. Fortunately, her sunburn already seemed better and the sunscreen seemed to have protected her from any more. After her shower she lathered on Taylor's after-sun treatment and, wrapped in a towel, she lay down for a little snooze. But she'd barely closed her eyes when she heard someone pounding on her door and then it opened.

"Lane!" she cried angrily, holding the towel protectively around her. "What are you doing?"

"Sorry." He turned around and looked the other way. "But I am so mad at Eliza and she was trying to throw me out. And no one else is home. I wondered if you could help a buddy out and—"

"What on earth are you saying?" DJ got to her feet, wrapping the towel more tightly around her just as Eliza burst in behind him.

"It figures I'd find you here," Eliza snapped at Lane. Then she looked at DJ. "And it figures you'd be practically naked."

"I took a shower!"

"Well, you two deserve each other!" Eliza shrieked. "And I'm going to tell Conner."

"Tell Conner what?" demanded DJ.

"Oh, just that I found you and Lane in your bedroom and that you were naked."

"I am NOT naked."

"You're not dressed either." Eliza laughed in a mean way. "In fact, I think I'll tell Conner how you got caught skinny dipping too. And how you and that sleazy security guard—"

"Eliza Wilton!" shouted Lane. "That's enough."

"Fine, take her side. Why should that surprise me!" Then Eliza stormed out.

"Please, leave," DJ said in a tight voice. "I would like to get dressed."

"I'm sorry, DJ. But Eliza was going nuts and she was trying to throw me out and I was waiting for Bradford to pick me up and—"

"Please, leave my room," DJ said firmly. "We can talk after I get dressed."

"So, you're not kicking me out of the house."

"Of course not!"

Fortunately, he left then. She quickly got dressed, then went out to see that Lane was sitting by himself in the living room. "Sorry about that," he told her sheepishly.

"What happened between you and Eliza?" DJ stood with her hands on her hips.

"She wanted to go clubbing tonight and I told her no."

"Oh ... " DJ considered this. "And that's what she was freaking over?"

He nodded. "Mostly."

"Look, if you can't be honest with—"

"Fine. I told her that I thought she needed to lay off the booze."

"And that flipped her out?"

"That and the fact that I mentioned how you and Taylor seem to get along fine without it. And how Harry has gotten on the wagon. And how maybe I'll get on it too."

"And that's what tripped her trigger."

"Mostly the part about you."

"About me?" DJ waited.

"I said something like, well, I can't remember it exactly."

"Come on," she urged him, "spit it out."

"I told Eliza it would be nice if she were more like you."

DJ closed her eyes and leaned her head back. "Thank you so very much."

"It was a compliment to you," he said quietly.

"It was like handing Eliza a loaded gun and telling her that it's now open season on DJ Lane."

He suddenly laughed.

"What is so funny?"

"I just figured it out."

"What?"

"We have the *same* name."

She just shook her head. "Not really. Lane is my last name."

"So if you married me, you'd be Mrs. Lane Lane?"

"No, it doesn't go like that. Besides I would *never* marry you."

He shook a finger at her. "Never say never, DJ."

"Okay, can we just set that aside for a moment? I need your help."

"You need my help?" He looked hopeful.

"Yes. I'm sure Eliza has already called Conner. And I'm going to call him and I know he'll believe me over her. But you need to convince him there's nothing between us too. Okay?"

"What if I don't believe that?"

"Just tell him the truth, okay?"

He shrugged. "Okay. Do you want me to call him now?"

"No, that will look contrived."

"Are you going to call him now?"

"I can't decide. I hate to act like I'm worried over Eliza's accusations, because I'm not. Mostly I'm just irritated."

"Don't let her get to you."

DJ laughed. "You're one to talk. Who came running into my room begging for help?"

"Eliza was acting like a crazy woman," he said defensively. "I thought maybe she was going to the kitchen for the butcher knife. I heard about a guy who got knifed by his girl on the news just—"

"Hello to the house," called out what sounded like Rhiannon's voice. "Anybody home?"

"In here," called DJ.

"What's up?" Bradford seemed to direct this to Lane. So while Lane gave them the lowdown on Eliza's temper tantrum, DJ went to get a soda in the kitchen.

"That's too bad about Eliza," Rhiannon said as she opened the fridge and pulled out a pitcher of iced tea.

"Tell me about it. I've just been elevated to Eliza's number-one enemy."

"Taylor will be so relieved."

Eliza spent the rest of Monday pouting. Probably exfoliating too since she wasn't too happy to see Casey showing up on Sunday evening looking far less orange than she was.

"I think DJ was right after all," Casey had told Eliza that night. "It seems like the saltwater actually helped tone down the dye."

"You and DJ can keep your freaking saltwater," Eliza had spat at her then stormed back to her room.

Finally, on Monday evening, Grandmother asked DJ to gather all the girls together for a last inspection. "If I have to cancel the photo shoot," she told her, "I'd at least like to give Josie some notice."

It was nearly ten o'clock when Grandmother had them line up in the kitchen for her examination. "You are still much too orange," she told Eliza with a scowl. "What do you plan to do about it?"

"I've done all the exfoliating my skin can handle," Eliza told her. "And I got some waterproof bronzer that I'll put on tomorrow."

Grandmother nodded. "Well, at least your hair looks pretty." She glanced at DJ. "Wish I could say the same for my own granddaughter."

Eliza snickered. "And check out her nails, Mrs. Carter."

"What have you been doing with these hands?" demanded Grandmother. "Laying cement?"

"Just surfing." DJ shrugged. "This is a swimsuit shoot, right?"

"Of course."

"What's wrong with looking like a surfer girl?"

Grandmother seemed to consider this as she fingered a lock of DJ's frazzled-looking hair. "Just the same, put some good conditioner on this hair tonight, do you understand?"

DJ just nodded.

Now Grandmother actually smiled at her. "At least you were right about that sunburn going away. You are a lovely shade of golden tan now."

"Just wait a few years," Eliza said cattily, "until the wrinkles and skin cancer kick in."

"I wonder what kind of carcinogen was in that orange dye," Taylor said evenly.

"Do you think?" asked Casey with concern.

"I've heard that it's a possibility."

Casey glared at Eliza. "That's the last time I listen to you!"

"Casey Atwood." Grandmother gave her a warning look, then softened. "Your coloring almost looks natural now. I think a little of Eliza's bronzer and you'll look just fine for tomorrow."

Next was Rhiannon. Grandmother twirled one of Rhiannon's red curls between her fingers then studied her pale freckled arm and smiled. "Perhaps Josie will appreciate that at least one of our girls may never be a poster child for skin cancer. It's actually refreshing to see how well you protect your skin, dear."

"Thanks."

"Now, Taylor." Grandmother's face lit up. "Pure perfection." She sighed. "Let's make sure that Josie sees you first, dear. That might put her at ease." Grandmother slapped her forehead now. "Good grief, why didn't we think to bring Daisy in Kriti's place? What was I thinking?"

"It'll be fine, Grandmother," DJ assured her.

"And I want you all to get a good night's sleep," she told them. "And make sure you drink a full glass of water before bed. With lemon in it." She shot out some more beauty commands, warned them against any shaving nicks, and finally told them there would be one last inspection tomorrow morning at seven o'clock sharp.

"But the shoot won't start until nine," complained DJ.

"I don't want you getting there with puffy eyes or sheet wrinkles on your cheeks."

"Sheet wrinkles?" DJ frowned.

"Someday you'll understand." Grandmother waved them off in a dismissive manner. "Go to bed!"

The location of the photo shoot was supposed to be top secret, but one of the girls (DJ suspected Casey) had spilled the beans and by noon, all the guys were hanging around the sidelines and watching. Taylor, Casey, and even Eliza, who now looked nearly as bronze as Taylor, seemed to enjoy the male attention, but Rhiannon and DJ wished they'd leave.

"Why are they here?" DJ complained for about the third time.

"Get over it already," Casey said in a blasé tone, like she was so used to this kind of thing.

"Maybe we should've sold tickets," DJ shot back as one of the stylists fluffed out her hair again.

"We want DJ and Taylor for the next one," Josie called out.

"Make it snappy, ladies, we're burning daylight," yelled the photographer.

Taylor and DJ jogged over to the edge of the water and waited for their direction. By now DJ knew better than to question them about anything. "Just pretend you're an actress," Taylor had whispered to her earlier. "You're on a stage and the director is calling the shots."

"Or maybe I'm a puppet," DJ had teased back. "I'll wait for them to pull my strings." It had taken about an hour for DJ to relax with it and finally she discovered a secret that worked. She just imitated Taylor. That seemed to make everyone happy. Or nearly. DJ was pretty certain there wasn't a thing, short of her jumping off a bridge, that would make Eliza happy.

"Yes!" yelled the photographer as Taylor and DJ began to splash in the wave that had just washed up. "That light is perfect, keep that going, girls!"

"Okay," called out Josie. "You girls go change into the next suits and hurry while we've still got this great afternoon light."

While the stylist helped DJ and Taylor change in the cabana, the other three girls went out to be photographed. After years of changing in locker rooms for sports, DJ had no problem stripping down. But she did have a problem with some of the swimsuits in Josie's lineup. Despite Grandmother's warning that the girls needed to do a bikini wax, DJ had drawn the line. "It was too painful," she'd explained to Josie earlier. "I'm sorry."

Fortunately, Josie had been so pleased with DJ's looks that she'd forgiven her lack of a bikini wax and allowed her to wear the less revealing suits as well as the board shorts. This pleased DJ and for that reason she was trying to be very cooperative.

"Ready?" DJ asked Taylor as the stylist made one last adjustment to her string bikini. "I hear the photographer yelling for us."

"This is beginning to feel like a sporting event," Taylor said as they jogged back out.

"You other girls can go now," Josie called as Casey, Rhiannon, and Eliza returned to the cabana.

"Us?" asked DJ hopefully.

"No, you and Taylor will stay. I think we can do the rest of the shots with just two girls." Josie waved at the others. "Thanks!"

And so, for the next hour or so, it was just the DJ and Taylor bikini madness marathon with the other three girls and Grandmother, plus the guys who continued to hoot and eventually drew an even bigger crowd, looking on. The whole while, Josie kept saying, "We're almost done, just a couple more shots," but it seemed to go on and on.

"There!" Josie finally proclaimed. "It's a wrap!"

"Whew." DJ paused to catch her breath. "That was harder than a soccer match."

"It's a good thing you're both athletic," Josie told them. "Some models would've bit the dust by now. You guys are real troopers."

"Thanks," Taylor told her.

"Thank you!" Now Josie turned to Grandmother, continuing to praise the girls' performances, particularly Taylor and DJ's, and promising to send some jpegs for their portfolios.

"Maybe we can finally leave now." Eliza spoke loudly—DJ figured it was to ensure that she and Taylor could hear as they changed back into their own clothes. "That is if the rock stars are ready to go. Or maybe they want to sign autographs for their fan club over there."

"Someone's jealous," whispered Taylor.

"No kidding." DJ pulled on her own board shorts and fastened them at the top, then slid her feet into her flip-flops. "I don't know about you, but I am due for an Eliza break."

"Or an Eliza breakdown." Taylor chuckled. "Seriously, that girl is strung so tight that I expect her to snap at any given moment."

"Well, let's not say or do anything to bring it on." DJ forced a smile as she and Taylor emerged from the cabana. "We're ready to go when you are," she told Eliza.

Eliza looked over to where Rhiannon and Casey had gone over to talk with the guys. "Now we'll need to drag them away." She let loose with a foul word. "The fun never quits."

Finally, it was decided that some of the girls would catch a ride with the boys. It was just DJ and Eliza riding home with Grandmother.

"What are we?" Eliza said sharply. "Like the lonely hearts club or something?"

Grandmother laughed. "Oh, my heart's not lonely, dear. In fact, the general just called and asked if we had room for him to join us for the weekend, and I told him that would be fine. I'll share Rhiannon's room and he can sleep in his own bed."

"Lovely." Eliza rolled her eyes.

DJ was tempted to say that she wasn't lonely either and that she had talked to Conner last night. She had assured him that Eliza was simply losing her mind and was so upset that Lane had broken up that she was trying to hurt anyone who crossed her path. Fortunately, Conner had believed DJ. But she could tell by the tone of his voice that he was concerned. "The big match is tomorrow," he'd finally told her. "But I've got a train ticket that leaves later that evening. I'll sleep on the train and get there early Thursday morning. Harry promised to pick me up."

DJ smiled to think of this now. She couldn't wait to see him.

"What's making you so smug?" Eliza asked her.

"Smug?" DJ looked at Eliza.

"Sitting there and smiling like the cat who swallowed the canary. Let me guess ... you're thinking at how great it is that you stole Lane from me."

"I didn't steal Lane from—"

"Girls!" Grandmother's voice was stern. "Please, do not argue about boys."

"We're not arguing," DJ told her. "I'm just telling Eliza that I have no interest in her ex-boyfriend. In fact, I was just thinking about Conner. He's going to be here Thursday morning."

"How nice." Grandmother nodded and smiled. "And you girls deserve to have some fun after the hard work you did today. Josie was quite pleased." She turned to DJ. "In fact, she seemed quite taken with you, DJ. I wasn't surprised that she was so pleased with Taylor. But it took me aback that she was so completely impressed with *you*. Can you believe she said she'd like to shoot you and Taylor for her next new line?"

"I think that's a great idea." Eliza aimed her forefinger at DJ like it was a gun, narrowed her eyes, clicked her thumb, then mouthed the word "bang!" Naturally, Grandmother wasn't looking her way. DJ laughed uneasily, but she did wonder—was Eliza really was losing it? Making threats? What was next?

15

spring breakdown

Everyone was in good spirits after the photo shoot on Tuesday. To celebrate their success Grandmother invited the boys to come over for a catered seafood dinner. "But no throwing the girls into the pool," she warned them before she headed off to her room to put her feet up. "The manager called after your Sunday night escapades and reminded me there are rules here." She looked directly at DJ. "I'm putting *you* in charge."

"Thanks a lot." DJ nodded to Taylor as Grandmother exited. "And because I know how to delegate, I'm putting *you* in charge."

"No problem." Taylor reached for another prawn. "Hey, where's Eliza? Doesn't she want to come out and get something to eat before it's too late?"

"She's probably pouting in her room," DJ said quietly.

"Actually, she's not," Casey informed them.

"So, she's not still mad at us?" asked DJ.

"I don't know about that, but I know she's not pouting in her room."

DJ studied Casey. "What are you saying?"

"That she's not here."

"Where is she?" asked Taylor curiously.

"On a date." Casey grinned mischievously.

DJ glanced around the patio. All the guys were present and accounted for. "On a date with who?"

"With *whom*." Taylor corrected her then laughed. "Yeah, who's she with, Case?"

"I'm not sure," Casey admitted.

"Then how do you know she's on a date?"

"I saw her getting ready."

"Getting ready for what?" asked DJ.

"To go out. *Duh*." Casey looked at DJ like she didn't have good sense.

"So much for the buddy system." DJ just shook her head.

"She's with a guy," Casey insisted. "Isn't that the same as a buddy?"

DJ was about to answer, but Seth was tugging Casey away. "Come on, my little Orange Crush." He pulled her to him like she was his personal plaything—like he owned her, body and soul. DJ turned away in disgust. Why did Casey put up with that?

"Who wants to go to a movie?" Taylor asked as she began reading the choices from the paper. It didn't take long for everyone to agree on a hot new release.

"I get to drive the general's car," Taylor announced.

"I'm going with her," Harry joked. Then Rhiannon and Bradford said they'd ride with them.

"And we'll go with Lane." Seth slipped his arm around Casey. "Ready, Babe?" She just smiled, nodding her head like a silly bobblehead doll.

"Looks like you're stuck with me," Lane told DJ with an apologetic smile.

"You know, I'm pretty tired," she said. "I think I'll pass on the movie this time." She glanced around the messy patio. "Besides, I need to clean this up."

"We can't leave you with all this mess," Lane said quickly. "I know." He reached into the pocket of his khaki shorts then tossed his keys to Seth. "You take my car and I'll stay here and help DJ."

And before she could make an argument, the others took off and it was just her and Lane—and, of course, Grandmother, although she was still off in her room. DJ went right to work clearing things and, to her relieved surprise, so did Lane. In less than an hour, the place was spotless. "You do good work," she told him.

"So East Coast boys are good for something."

She laughed. "Want to see if there's anything good on TV?" DJ handed him the remote then settled into a comfy club chair (avoiding the sectional where he was seated) and waited as he flipped through the channels. She knew that what they were doing was completely innocent, but she also knew that someone like Eliza could pop in and jump to all kinds of conclusions. Not that she expected to see Eliza any time soon. DJ's guess was that Eliza had gone out with one of the admirers from the photo shoot—probably clubbing. Not that DJ thought that was a smart thing to do or that Grandmother would approve. Anyway, it seemed unlikely that Eliza would be home soon.

Finally it was getting late and DJ really was tired. "Do you mind if I call it a night?" she asked him sleepily.

"Not if you don't mind me crashing here until the guys get back with my car."

She glanced at the clock then shrugged. "They should be back pretty soon anyway." She told him good night, trudged to her room, crashed in bed, and fell sound asleep.

DJ was the first one up the next morning. She tiptoed to the bathroom where she tugged on her swimsuit, then quietly crept back through the room again, trying to avoid waking Taylor. DJ had to smile to remember the old times and how she used to stomp around and make noise when Taylor was sleeping off a hangover. Thankfully those days were gone. At least she hoped so. DJ actually bent down to look at Taylor, even sniffing to be sure. Convinced that all was well, DJ quietly went out the patio doors and then slipped into the pool to swim laps. It felt delicious to slice through the smooth water. She had the pool to herself and nothing to think about but the day ahead. Maybe she'd go surfing again if she could talk Casey into joining her.

Finally, satisfied with her workout, she climbed out and sat on the edge of the pool. Unfortunately she'd forgotten to bring a towel, and before long she was shivering in the cool morning air. Just as she was about to get up, she felt someone draping a towel around her shoulders. Thinking it was Taylor she turned around with a smile. "Lane?" she said in surprise. "What are you doing here?"

He gave her lopsided grin. "I actually spent the night."

"What?"

"Seth pulled a jerk stunt last night."

"Huh?"

"He and Casey never even went to the movie. Harry tried to call him, but his phone was off. So Taylor drove the guys back to my grandparents' place, thinking I'd be there. Naturally, I wasn't. So I got stuck here all night. Taylor said it was okay. Hope you don't mind."

She stood up and stomped a bare foot onto the cement. "Actually I do mind. I mind a lot!"

"Sorry." He stepped back.

"No, I don't mean you. I understand that. What ticks me off is Casey. I can't believe she'd pull something like that here. My grandmother will be furious if she finds out."

"Will she find out?"

DJ bit her lower lip.

"And to be fair, it might not be completely Casey's fault. That Seth . . . well, I don't like to dis on friends—not that he's such a great friend, taking off with my car and all. But I don't totally trust the guy."

DJ nodded vigorously. "That's how I feel."

"Anyway, if you wouldn't mind, I could use a lift back to my place. It's only about five miles. I thought about walking."

"Just let me get dressed," she said as she took off back to her room. Taylor was still asleep and DJ quietly got dressed, grabbed her bag, and met up with Lane in the kitchen. "Let me leave a note for Grandmother, just in case." She quickly scrawled something and then they left.

"I know Seth might be a jerk," she told Lane as she drove, "but it totally irks me that Casey just lets him control her. She never used to be like that."

"Sometimes girls change for guys," he said in a philosophical way, "and sometimes guys change for girls."

"Isn't it better just to be ourselves?"

"Turn left on the next street." He sighed. "What if the changes we make for someone else are improvements, like Harry?"

DJ nodded. "I have to admit I like Harry a lot more now that he's quit drinking."

"And, don't take this wrong, DJ, but you've been a good influence on me."

She glanced over uneasily. "Meaning?"

"I like the way you embrace life—the way you're so comfortable in your own skin, and that you don't need to drink to have a good time."

DJ wasn't sure that all that was true, but she thanked him anyway.

"It's this development," he told her. Then they passed through security and he directed her to his grandparents' house.

"Do you mind if I go in and drag out Casey?"

"You really want to do that?"

She considered a confrontation with Seth and Casey, probably both hung over and probably not too happy to see her. "Maybe not."

"How about if I bring her back later?"

"Will you check on her?" DJ asked quietly. "I mean—to see that she's okay."

He nodded. "Sure."

Then she thanked him and drove back to the general's house. And, yes, a part of her did feel sorry for Casey. But another part of her just didn't get it. Why was Casey being such a fool? And why did Casey pick such loser guys? First she'd been with Garrison, which had been a train wreck from the get-go. Then she hooked up with Seth—knowing full well how it had been with him and Taylor before Taylor wised up and got sober. Maybe some girls had to be kicked around before they figured things out. DJ was thankful she wasn't one of them. But, she knew that old saying, "but by the grace of God . . ." And so, as she drove, she prayed for Casey. She begged God to shake that girl up and straighten her out before her life got completely derailed.

The house was still quiet when she got back, and now DJ wondered if she should tell her grandmother. But then she wondered … what good would it do? DJ tiptoed back to her room and was relieved to see that Taylor was awake now.

"Where have you been?" Taylor was just out of the shower, tying the belt of her bathrobe and shaking out her damp hair.

DJ quickly explained the situation. "I'm getting seriously worried about Casey," she said finally. "It's like she's on a path to self-destruct."

"That's a path I know well." Taylor sighed as she towel dried her hair.

"Lane promised to check on her and bring her back. And now I'm trying to decide whether to tell my grandmother … not that it will help matters."

"Why don't we just talk to Casey?" suggested Taylor. "Do another intervention of sorts. And you can always hold telling your grandmother over her head. I mean, if she wants to keep doing stupid stuff."

"It's worth a try."

But when Lane brought Casey home, it was obvious that she wasn't in any kind of condition to talk. "Let's give her time," Taylor advised DJ as they watched Casey staggering down the hallway to her room. "That girl isn't going anywhere for a while."

"And if it makes you feel any better," Lane told them, "I read Seth the riot act. I told him he could pack his stuff and leave if he pulls a stunt like that again."

"Did he listen?" asked DJ.

"Oh, yeah." Lane nodded. "The other guys backed me up. We told him we'd throw him out."

"Thanks." DJ sighed. "Well, I guess I won't be surfing today."

"Why not?" asked Lane.

"Well, I'd been hoping Casey would—"

"I know I'm not as good a surfer as you," he said quickly, "but I rented my board for the week."

"So did I." DJ glanced at Taylor now. "Should I go?"

"Why not?" Taylor nodded. "You stayed home and cleaned up last night, Cinderella, so it seems like you should have some fun today."

"What about Casey?"

Taylor narrowed her eyes. "You don't think I can handle that girl?"

DJ laughed. "I know you can. Probably better than any of us."

"Leave Casey to me today. You go and have some fun."

So that was just what DJ did. And what a great day for surfing it was—a perfectly delicious sort of day with blue sky and sun and good long rides on fast-moving waves. Only one thing could have made this day better, and DJ knew that he would be here tomorrow!

16

spring breakdown

DJ had barely walked in the door of the general's beach house when she sensed something was wrong. She could hear Rhiannon and Taylor talking quietly in the kitchen, but the tone of their voices sounded worried and somewhat urgent.

"What's going on?" DJ asked. "Is Casey okay?"

"Casey's just starting to feel better," Rhiannon told her with worried eyes.

"Yeah, after barfing her guts out for most of the day." Taylor shook her head sadly.

"Maybe this will make her think twice before she does—"

"Casey isn't our biggest concern right now," Taylor interrupted.

"What do you mean?"

"Eliza never came home last night either."

DJ let out an exasperated sigh.

"We didn't actually figure this out until just a little while ago," admitted Rhiannon.

"It looked like her bed had been slept in," Taylor told her, "so we just assumed that she'd come home and taken off again—probably with her mystery man."

"Then we realized that it was possible that Eliza hadn't made her bed from the night before."

"But you don't know that for sure," DJ pointed out. "Maybe she did get home last night. Casey wasn't there to see her, right?"

"That's true." Taylor nodded. "But we snooped around and it just doesn't seem like she came home last night."

"We think we would've seen her clubbing clothes," Rhiannon said. "Because Eliza isn't exactly tidy after a night out."

"And the shower would've been used," Taylor said, "because Eliza wouldn't think of going out again without a shower, but it was dry and no wet towels."

"That is strange."

"We could be wrong . . . " Taylor paused at the sound of footsteps and then Grandmother entered the kitchen.

"Oh, I'm glad you girls are here," she said. "I was thinking this might be a nice evening to go out for dinner. The general told me about a lovely little restaurant over on—"

"I, uh, I don't think so." DJ tried to think of some good reason, but came up blank.

Grandmother scowled. "Why not?"

"Because we already ordered pizza," Taylor said quickly.

"Pizza?" Grandmother looked disappointed.

"Besides, we're kind of tired," DJ said. "It's been a long day."

"Are the boys coming over again?" she asked.

"Not tonight," Rhiannon answered. "I think we all need a night off."

"Maybe we can do something special tomorrow," DJ offered. "Conner will be here then."

Grandmother just nodded. "Yes, I suppose that's a good plan." She turned to open the refrigerator and looked in.

Taylor held up her hand like a phone and mouthed the word *pizza*. DJ nodded. And Rhiannon made the phone gesture too. *Boys*, she mouthed. DJ nodded again.

"Perhaps I'll just finish off some of these seafood leftovers from last night . . . " said Grandmother. "If no one minds."

"Help yourself," DJ called out as she left the kitchen, heading for Casey's room. Her plan was to get Casey to divulge more information about the whereabouts of Miss Eliza Wilton.

"Hey, Casey," she said as she walked right in without knocking. "I hear you're feeling better."

Casey was sitting in a chair by the window, but she looked kind of limp and wiped out. "Uh-huh."

DJ sat down on the end of one of the beds and considered her words. Part of her wanted to tear into Casey and give her a solid piece of her mind. But another part of her knew that could backfire. What DJ needed now was information. And it seemed the only one who knew anything would be Casey.

"So, Casey," she began carefully, "I hear that Eliza never came home last night either."

Casey nodded then put her hand to her forehead like it hurt. "That's what Taylor and Rhiannon seem to think," she said in a hoarse voice.

"But you don't?"

She shrugged. "I don't know."

"Because you weren't here either."

Casey looked down at her lap.

"Anyway . . . it seems you were the last one to talk to Eliza. You said she was going out on a date, right?"

"Right."

"You assumed to a club?"

159

"Yeah. She was dressing up."

"Do you remember what she wore?"

Casey frowned. "Not exactly."

"Do you remember anything she said about who she was going with?"

Casey leaned over and put her head in her hands. "I don't feel so good."

"Are you going to throw up again?"

Casey didn't answer and DJ was afraid she was about to say something stupid and so she stood up. "Sorry you're sick," she said stiffly. "Seems like you might want to think about that—" Then Casey took off for the bathroom and DJ left.

"Pizza is coming," Taylor told DJ when she came back out.

"And I called the guys and told them that Eliza might be missing," Rhiannon said, "and Bradford said they'd be on the lookout for her."

"Should I tell Grandmother?" asked DJ.

Rhiannon nodded. "Probably."

"It did occur to me that she could be pulling the same kind of thing I did last fall," Taylor said. "Remember my little disappearing act after Casey humiliated me on MySpace?"

DJ nodded eagerly. "She could be doing something like that. It wouldn't surprise me. She might be in some swanky hotel being waited on and ordering room service and just letting us freak."

Rhiannon brightened. "You know, that does sound possible."

"But what if we're wrong?" asked DJ.

"What do we know for sure?" said Taylor as she reached for a notepad. "Let's write it down."

"Her phone is turned off," said Rhiannon. "It goes straight to messaging and she hasn't returned our calls."

"What did she take with her?" asked DJ suddenly. "I mean, if she was going to hole up in a hotel, wouldn't she take an overnight bag or some personal items?"

"Unless she wanted to make it look like she was simply missing," said Taylor.

"Did Casey see anyone picking Eliza up?" asked Rhiannon.

"Casey can't remember anything at the moment," DJ said. "She hardly knows her own name."

"Very helpful."

DJ thought hard for a moment and suddenly knew what had to be done. "Whether or not Eliza is jerking us around, I need to inform my grandmother."

"I think so too," admitted Rhiannon.

"I agree." Taylor nodded. "Just in case something really is wrong."

"Like what if she's been kidnapped?" Rhiannon's eyes got wide.

"It doesn't seem likely, but you never know." DJ was trying to think of an easy way to break this news to Grandmother.

Taylor suddenly pointed out toward the pool. "Although there are definitely some pervs around—you never know."

"Is our sleazy friend out there again?" asked DJ.

"No, it's a different guy tonight."

"Good. They probably gave the other jerk the boot." DJ braced herself. "Well, I'm going to speak to Grandmother. Anyone else want to come?"

They both shook their heads no, so DJ went alone. She knocked on the door, waited to be asked in, and then quickly broke the news. "Eliza seems to be missing, Grandmother."

"Missing?" She looked up from where she'd been eating at a small table by a window.

So DJ gave the details, or as many details as she could remember. Grandmother's face grew cloudy with concern. She pushed the plate away and closed her eyes as if she wanted to shut out this bad news.

"I realize that Eliza might just be pulling a stunt," DJ said finally, "but I felt you should know."

Grandmother's eyes opened wide. "Of course I should know. How long have you known she was missing?"

"Not even an hour."

"Oh. And she's been missing since yesterday evening?"

DJ nodded.

"Oh." Now Grandmother looked seriously disturbed. "What shall we do, DJ? Do we call her parents?"

"Aren't they in Nepal?"

Grandmother nodded eagerly. "Yes, you're right. They are in Nepal. And I'm sure we can't reach them there. Not yet anyway."

"So, I guess we simply deal with it."

Grandmother stood now. "Do you think that nasty security man might be involved?"

"Taylor wondered that same thing. But Casey had thought Eliza was going out last night."

"Going out with whom?"

"We don't know. Casey said that Eliza was dressed up for a date."

"Did someone pick Eliza up?"

"Not that we know of."

"Perhaps Eliza left the house, dressed up ... and was abducted by that horrible security guard!"

"I—uh—I don't know."

But Grandmother was already on the phone. "Yes, this is an emergency," she was telling someone. "We have a missing girl and I need to speak to whoever is in charge immediately." Then she gave the address and hung up. "They are on their way."

Pizza and the security guard arrived simultaneously. But as Rhiannon and Taylor dealt with the pizza guy, Grandmother and DJ talked to the security guard. DJ filled in the details, answering his questions as best she could.

"You can call the police," he told them, "but they may not put out a missing persons report for another day or two. In the meantime, I'll put my guys on it around here."

"Speaking of your guys," Grandmother began, "we have cause for concern that one of them may be involved."

The security guard frowned. "What are you suggesting?"

So Grandmother quickly told the story about the incident at the pool.

"Oh, you're the ones that called up about Tom?"

"Tom?"

"The security guard that tried to get the naked girl out of the pool after hours."

"Naked girl?" Grandmother looked stunned.

"Yeah, apparently there were a couple of them, skinny dipping." He frowned at DJ. "You know anything about that?"

She just nodded.

"So, tell me, was the other girl the one that's missing—this Eliza Wilton?"

"No, it was someone else," Grandmother said quietly.

"How many girls you got, lady?"

She blinked. "Just five. One didn't come."

"What kind of a place are you running here anyway?"

Now Grandmother was offended. "What kind of security are you running?" she asked him bluntly.

"Naked girls in the pool, running away ... " He shook his head. "Sounds like spring break to me. I doubt anyone in law enforcement will take any of this too seriously."

"Well, thank you for your time," Grandmother said crisply.

"I'll let you know if we find any lost or naked girls," he said with a chuckle.

"Wait a minute," DJ said quickly. "What about that security guard—you said his name is Tom. Did he get fired?"

"Fired?" He laughed. "No."

"Where is he then?"

"It's his day off. He gets Wednesdays and Thursdays off."

"Oh ... "

"Anything else I can do for you?"

"What's his last name?" DJ demanded.

"Tom?" He thought for a minute. "Oh, yeah. Jones."

"His name is *Tom Jones*?" Grandmother looked skeptical.

"Yeah, he gets teased about it sometimes. He can't sing to save his life."

Grandmother began to pace as soon as the security guard left. DJ could tell that she was angry ... and worried.

"I'm sorry about the skinny-dipping thing," DJ told her. "It seemed like a good idea at the time."

Grandmother let out an exasperated sigh. "I don't know what to do. I just do not know what to do."

"Should we call the police?" asked DJ. "That security guard didn't sound too smart to me. I'm not sure we should take his advice."

"Yes. Good point." Grandmother nodded. "Get me the phone."

"Wait," said DJ. "What about the FBI?"

"Even better!"

DJ listened as Grandmother explained the situation to the person on the other end, but some of her details weren't quite accurate. "May I speak to them?" DJ whispered.

"My granddaughter wants to talk." She shoved the phone at DJ and DJ tried to correct some of the information. "But that's not all," she said finally. "I thought you should know that the girl who is missing is from one of the wealthiest families in the country. She's an heiress."

"Are you sure about this?" asked the woman on the other end.

"Positive. You can ask my grandmother if you like."

Grandmother was nodding eagerly now, reaching for the phone. DJ handed it back and Grandmother made it very clear that they were, indeed, looking for a very wealthy young woman. Finally, she hung up and collapsed into a nearby chair, patting her chest as if she were about to expire.

"Are you okay?" DJ leaned over to peer into her grandmother's pale blue eyes.

"Yes. Just rattled. And thank you, DJ. I think we may have gotten their attention."

"I guess it's true that money talks."

"They asked if we have a recent photo."

DJ thought hard. "Hey, maybe Josie could email one from yesterday's photo shoot."

"Yes, yes. Good thinking. I'll call her right now."

By eleven o'clock, they had done all they knew how to do and everyone was thoroughly concerned. "We could go out looking for her," offered DJ.

"No!" Grandmother firmly shook her head. "Absolutely not! I will not risk losing any more girls, thank you very much."

"The guys have been out looking," Rhiannon told her.

"Where is Casey?" demanded Grandmother suddenly. "Please, do not tell me she's gone missing too."

"She's asleep," DJ said quickly. "She wasn't feeling too well today."

"She's probably worried about Eliza," Grandmother suggested.

DJ just nodded, exchanging glances with Taylor and Rhiannon.

"I see no reason for us to stay up all night." Grandmother stood. "For now I am going with Taylor's theory . . . let's just hope that Eliza is simply hiding out in some five star hotel. It was obvious that she felt slighted at the photo shoot yesterday and I can understand her disappointment about losing her boyfriend's affections. That could explain a lot." She shook her head. "Even so, I will not tolerate this sort of behavior. If Eliza is playing us for fools, she will be going home to her parents as soon as we find her. Because I am too old for these kinds of shenanigans. I am fed up." Then she marched off to bed.

17

spring breakdown

"What if Tom Jones really did kidnap Eliza?" Taylor said this after Grandmother was out of earshot. "If that really is his name, which I seriously doubt."

"It does seem fishy that Eliza disappears the same time he gets his days off." Rhiannon stared out at the quiet pool. "And I wonder what kind of police checks are done on security guards."

"He did creep me out." DJ shuddered to remember the sleazy sound of his voice as he tried to entice her to come out of the pool. "Eliza might not be my best friend, but I sure hope she's not with Tom Jones right now."

"Your grandmother's right," Taylor said. "It won't do any good to stay up worrying. And maybe tomorrow we'll think of something."

"Or Eliza will decide to come home," offered Rhiannon sadly.

"I think we should pray for her," said DJ so suddenly that she actually surprised herself. "God knows where she is and what she needs."

"I have been praying," admitted Taylor. "But you're right. We should all pray together." And so they did pray. They took turns asking God to watch over Eliza, to keep her safe, and to get her back to them as soon as possible. And then they went to bed. But a whole hour passed and DJ was unable to sleep. Then suddenly she heard someone opening the door to their bedroom. She froze and prepared herself to scream.

"I'm afraid," whispered a quiet voice that sounded like Casey.

"What?" DJ sat up and turned the light on.

"What is it?" said Taylor.

"Casey just scared the bajeebers out of me."

"I'm sorry, but I was scared being alone. I got to thinking about those security guards and how they might have keys to this place and be able to sneak in here and ... anyway, can I sleep with you guys?"

DJ threw back her blanket. "Come on in."

"Thanks." Casey hopped into bed.

"I can't stop thinking about her," DJ whispered. "Wondering where she is and if she's okay."

"Me too," Casey whispered back.

"We need some kind of clues," Taylor said quietly.

"Does anyone remember a specific guy that she was talking to at the photo shoot?"

No one said anything.

"Can you remember anything that she said to you that evening, Casey? Did she mention the guy's name or whether he lived around here or how old he was or where they might've been going?" persisted Taylor.

"Okay, I'm trying really hard to remember," Casey said quietly. "She was getting dressed ... and she changed a couple of times ... "

"Like she really cared about how she looked." Taylor sat up and turned on the light. "Let's write this down, okay?" She ran for the notepad she'd already been using to write down clues.

"So what did she finally wear?" asked DJ.

Casey frowned as if straining her brain. "It was a Betsey Johnson dress," she said suddenly. "Now I remember. She bought it the first day we were here. We went into a Betsey Johnson shop, which I thought was dumb, but I didn't say so. And she tried on some dresses and ended up getting this black and pale pink one. Strapless and pretty dressy."

"So she was going clubbing in style," Taylor said as she wrote something down. Just then the door to their bedroom opened and they all jumped.

"I'm sorry," Rhiannon said. "But I saw the lights on and heard you and wondered if everything was okay."

"Join the party," said DJ.

"We're trying to get Casey's memory to kick in," Taylor told her. "So far we know that Eliza went out in a new dress."

"And that she changed outfits a few times, so she was obviously trying to impress this guy."

"But who *is* this guy?" asked Rhiannon as she sat down at the end of DJ's bed. "Can you remember anything, Casey?"

"Come on," persisted DJ. "Didn't she say anything about the guy? We know Eliza likes to brag. And weren't you curious? I mean, you knew she and Lane were history. So didn't you even ask? Like maybe he was an Ivy Leaguer or some rich guy from Louisville. What was the connection?"

Casey slowly nodded. "Yeah, I did ask her. I was curious. And she was being all mysterious about it. Like she didn't want anyone to know too much. She even said she was keeping this guy to herself this time. Like she was afraid one of us would steal him."

"Did she say a name? Or describe him or anything?" asked Taylor.

Casey jumped out of bed now. "I remember something. She said *I knew him!*"

"That you knew him?" DJ was confused.

"Yes. She was acting really coy about it and she said that I'd already met him and that I'd thought he was good looking too."

"So think really hard to the photo shoot, Case," DJ urged her. "Who did you meet there that seemed interested in Eliza? Who did you think was good looking?"

Casey's face went blank. "I honestly don't remember meeting anyone. I mostly hung with Seth whenever I had a free moment. He wasn't too thrilled with our little fan club and he would've been ticked if I'd talked to those guys."

"Then who would it be that you could possibly know? We know who's here from school. It couldn't be one of them." Taylor went over the guys. "Seth was with Casey. Bradford and Harry were with Rhiannon and me. And Lane?" She looked at DJ. "He was here, with you, right?"

"Yeah." DJ glanced at Casey. "Thanks to Seth never coming back."

"So, anyway, Lane was with you all night."

"Wait a minute." DJ held up her hands. "He wasn't with me all night. I went to bed. He slept in the living room."

"I saw him when I first came home, but I don't remember seeing him after that." Taylor turned to Rhiannon. "Did you?"

"I went straight to bed."

Taylor nodded. "Me too. And the lights were off."

"Do you think Lane has something to do with it?" asked Casey.

"No way." DJ firmly shook her head. "That's ridiculous."

"But we all knew that he and Eliza weren't getting along," Casey pointed out. "They'd had a big fight just the day before."

"He had opportunity and motive." Taylor held up two fingers.

"Sure thing, Sherlock," said DJ. "But get serious. Are you suggesting that Lane took Eliza out and murdered her?"

"Maybe Eliza came in and picked a fight with him," said Casey suddenly. "She could've been drinking and ... you know ... "

"She might've thought he was spending the night with you," Taylor pointed to DJ. "And she flew into a jealous rage and to quiet her down, Lane took her outside and—"

"This is totally absurd." DJ held up her hands. "Lane is so not like that."

"You're certainly jumping to his defense," said Casey.

DJ turned to Casey. "Look, if it was Seth, I might wonder. I was actually pretty worried about you—"

"Seth would never hurt me!"

"Okay, okay." Taylor made a time-out sign. "Let's not start attacking each other."

"I have to agree with DJ on this," said Rhiannon. "I do not think Lane murdered Eliza."

DJ rolled her eyes. "Great. Maybe we should all go to sleep now."

Rhiannon grabbed Casey's hand. "You have to room with me tonight. I'm too scared to sleep alone."

Finally, with the room quiet and the lights off, DJ thought maybe she could go to sleep. But as she was drifting, she ran the things that she'd heard tonight through her head. Not the stupid accusation against Lane. That really was preposterous. But the other clues ... she let them tumble about as she prayed for Eliza again and eventually fell asleep.

"I have an idea!" DJ shouted as she woke up the next morning. It was barely even light out, but she was wide awake and her mind was racing.

"What's going on?" Taylor asked sleepily.

"I have an idea about who Eliza's mystery man might be."

Taylor sat up and blinked. "Okay, don't keep me in suspense."

"Remember that guy we met on the plane?" DJ jumped out of bed and dashed to Rhiannon's room and burst in. "Wake up!"

Soon they were all awake and DJ was spilling out her theory. "Remember that guy who was flirting with us on the plane?" She nodded to Taylor. "He was trying to get us to tell him our final destination. He wanted to buy us drinks."

Taylor nodded. "He even told us his name." She scratched her head. "What was it?"

"Oh, yeah," Casey nodded. "He talked to us too. He was going to Fort Lauderdale for spring break. Eliza told him we were going to Palm Beach."

"So, see." DJ pointed at Casey. "That's a guy that you met."

"That's right." Casey frowned. "He told us his name ... What was it?"

"He told us too." Taylor closed her eyes. "He was a little over six feet tall. He had brown eyes ... "

"And blond hair," added DJ.

"No, it was naturally brown," Taylor corrected. "The tips were bleached."

"Yeah, I think you're right," agreed DJ.

"And he was trying to guess where we were headed ... " Taylor's brow creased. "And his name started with a J. Like Josh or Justin or Jared or ... "

"Jeremy!" DJ said suddenly. "I remember because my first boyfriend's name was Jeremy! Remember, Casey?"

Casey looked confused. "No, I don't think that's right. I think he told us his name was something different. Something shorter. Todd!" she said suddenly. "His name was Todd."

"Great," said Taylor. "We don't even have a name."

"Maybe he was lying about his name," said DJ. "Maybe he was already up to something."

"Good point." Taylor turned back to Casey. "You're sure it was Todd?"

Casey nodded. "I'm positive. I used to read a series of books where the main guy was named Todd. He was a cool dude. I think I figured this Todd was okay too."

"And he offered you guys drinks?" asked DJ.

"Naturally, we declined."

"Naturally."

"But!" Casey was on her feet now. "Eliza gave Todd, or whatever his name is, her phone number. She said maybe he could buy us a drink in Palm Beach if he ever made it up here."

"She gave a complete stranger her phone number?" DJ wanted to scream.

"He wasn't a complete stranger," Casey argued. "He did introduce himself."

"With a phony name." DJ scowled.

"I've done the same thing myself," Taylor admitted. "Not that I'm proud of it and I wouldn't do it again."

"So what do we really know?" asked Rhiannon.

Taylor had her pad out again.

"We know that Eliza gave this Todd/Jeremy dude her phone number." DJ held up one finger. "And we know that Eliza told Casey she was going out with someone Casey had met." She held up two fingers. "And we know that Eliza trusted this guy enough to get dressed up for him." She held up three fingers and then stopped.

"And we know she never came home afterward."

"Girls! Girls!" called Grandmother urgently. "Desiree? Taylor? Where are you girls?"

"In here," DJ called down the hallway. "What's wrong?"

Grandmother looked seriously rattled now. She was in her pajamas with only one slipper on and her hair sticking out like a scarecrow. "A phone call," she gasped as she came into the room and sank down on a bed. "A man on the other end."

"What did he say?" demanded DJ.

"I'll write it down," said Taylor.

"He said"—Grandmother paused for a breath—"that he had Eliza. He said"—she paused again—"that he wanted ransom money."

"What else?" asked DJ.

"He said not to call the police." She looked truly frightened now. "Or that something terrible would happen."

"And you didn't call the police, Grandmother. You called the FBI."

Grandmother nodded. "That's right. I did."

"Did he say anything else, Mrs. Carter?" asked Taylor eagerly.

"He said he would be in touch with details."

"And?" persisted DJ.

"Then he hung up."

"Probably didn't want to be traced," said DJ. "Which phone did he call on? Your cell?"

"No, the one in the bedroom."

"He knows the landline number," DJ said to Taylor.

"Eliza must've told him."

"We need to call the FBI," said Taylor.

Suddenly Grandmother was crying. "I cannot do this. I am too old. Oh, what was I thinking to bring a bunch of girls down here?" She leaned over and sobbed even harder.

"It's going to be okay," DJ told her calmly.

"Come on," said Rhiannon in a soothing voice. "I'll walk you back to your room, Mrs. Carter. DJ will call the FBI. We have some new clues to tell them. Now you just breathe deeply, okay?"

DJ told Rhiannon thanks and reached for her cell phone, which she'd kept by her side all night. Taylor was ready with the number and DJ even remembered the name of the woman they'd talked with yesterday. "May I please speak to Marsha Stein?" she asked politely. She was given another number, which Taylor wrote down, and soon she had Marsha on the other end. DJ quickly filled her in on the phone call.

"Which number did he call on?"

DJ gave her the landline number. "Unfortunately it's an old-fashioned phone and doesn't have caller ID."

"He's probably using a blocked number anyway. But did you push star fifty-seven to trace it back?"

"No, should we?"

"No, but don't touch that landline phone in case we can trace it back. Mostly, you don't want to rattle this guy right now."

"And we have even more information." DJ told Marsha about the guy on the plane. About him giving them different names and finally about Eliza sharing her phone number with him. "We think it's likely this is the same guy," DJ told her. "Because Eliza told her roommate that it was someone she'd met. And it just seems to be the only possibility."

Marsha asked for the flight information, Eliza's cell phone number, and a description of the Todd/Jeremy character. "This will be very helpful," she told DJ.

"What do we do now?" DJ asked. "I mean, what if the guy calls again?"

"For now, you just sit tight. I'm sending someone to your address as we speak. His name is Dan Jackson, he'll show you his ID and then he'll set up a wire tap. In the meantime I'll be checking the passenger list for the Fort Lauderdale flight as well as Eliza's cell phone records, and with any luck I might have some photos for you girls to identify."

"Thanks!"

"Thank you. That's some good information you just gave me. If we can put the pieces together we might be able to catch this guy."

DJ closed her phone and filled in Taylor and Casey. "I'm going to check on my grandmother," she told them. "I've never seen her fall apart like that before. It's got me worried."

Casey nodded. "Yeah, me too."

DJ found Grandmother back in her bed with Rhiannon tending to her. "She asked for a bottle of pills that were in her purse," Rhiannon whispered. "They were tranquilizers—prescribed to her. I only gave her one. It didn't seem like it could hurt."

"Probably not." DJ went over and smiled at Grandmother. "Good news."

"They found Eliza?"

"Not quite. But they have a lot of clues now. They don't think it'll be long."

Grandmother closed her eyes. "Oh, good … "

"You just rest," DJ told her. "We'll keep you posted."

"I called the general," she said sleepily. "He's catching an earlier flight … should be here this evening."

"Good." DJ actually felt relieved. "We could use his help right now."

"Oh, yes." She sighed sleepily. "We certainly could."

DJ quietly left her grandmother's room. But once she was outside, she felt like she was close to tears too. Really, this was too much for them to deal with. They needed someone like the general. Or even DJ's father. Not that she planned to call him. Even if he was concerned, what could he do? She leaned against the wall and realized that the only father figure she could really rely on was God. And so, once again, she prayed. She prayed for Eliza and then she prayed for the rest of them. "Please, help us," she finally whispered. "Amen."

"Praying?" asked Rhiannon as she came out of Grandmother's room.

DJ nodded.

"Me too."

"Thanks for helping with her." DJ nodded toward the closed door.

"No problem. She and I are actually starting to bond."

DJ smiled. "And I know that's not easy." Just then her cell phone rang and, to her relief, it was Conner.

"Hey, I just heard about Eliza. Is there anything I can do?"

DJ gave him the latest, saying how the FBI guy was on his way. "In fact, it sounds like someone's at the door now."

"Be careful," he warned. "Don't let just anyone in."

"We'll check ID."

"Why don't I stay on the phone," he said quickly. "Just until you make sure it's really the FBI."

"Thanks." She hurried to the front door in time to see Taylor checking the FBI badge of a tall black guy in a navy suit. "Okay, Dan Jackson, you seem to be the real deal. Come on in."

DJ nodded to Taylor. "And just in case he's not, I've got the authorities here on the phone."

"Is that Marsha?" he asked hopefully.

DJ grinned. "No, I was just checking."

He nodded. "Smart girl."

"The phone's in here." Taylor led him into the living room.

"The guy's legit," DJ told Conner now. "But thanks for staying on the line."

"So what can we do to help?" asked Conner.

"For starters, just get over here."

"Will do. But all the guys are with me. You want us all over there?"

"Sure. Maybe we can form a search party."

As DJ hung up, she thought that might not be such a bad idea. She went over to the general's computer and went online to see if Eliza had a spot on any of the social networks. Sure enough, she had a couple. DJ quickly downloaded and printed some photos.

"What are you doing?" asked Casey.

DJ showed her. "Now how about the Betsey Johnson dress ... do you think you can find it online?"

Casey went to work and within minutes had a several copies of the dress printed out. "Here you go."

DJ took the photos to Dan Jackson and explained them.

"Good stuff," he told her. "Marsha is on her way over."

"We've got a bunch of guys on their way too," DJ told him. "But maybe it's going to be too crowded here. Still, they're willing to do some looking around town."

"And we might have more information soon. As long as they can lie low and be quiet while we're working."

Marsha made it there before the guys. And she had photos. "Thanks to post-nine-eleven security," she told the girls, "no one gets on a plane without photo ID or getting their photo taken." She tossed a pile of photocopied pages on the dining room table. "You girls get to work."

Despite the grainy quality of the black-and-white photos, they all agreed on one. "This is him," Casey told Marsha. "Not Todd or Jeremy, it seems."

Marsha read the name. "Theodore Wayne Johnston from Newark." She handed the page off to Dan now. "Can you do a search on him, see if he's got a record? I'll get someone at the office to check for a rental car and phone records."

"Wow," said Casey, "this is moving along."

"Don't be fooled," Marsha said as she punched some things into her laptop. "This is the easy part. After that it can be like a needle in a haystack." She turned to DJ now. "And I assume Theodore, or shall we call him Ted, hasn't called since the first time."

"No."

Just then the guys arrived and, after Conner and DJ exchanged a long hug, she ushered them all into the kitchen where she dispensed the latest information.

"We thought we could take Eliza's photos and ask around at some of the local hot spots," Lane told DJ. "Places where all the spring break parties are going on."

"We already accused Lane of wanting to check out the hot babes," teased Seth. "You know that whole girls gone wild thing." He nudged Casey like this was funny and she just glared at him. "Excuse me," he said sarcastically.

"If we had another car, we could split up," Conner told DJ. "That way we could cover a lot more territory."

"Sounds like a plan," DJ agreed.

"I'll print some more photos," Casey said. "We could even put a lost girl thing together with a phone number to call."

"Great idea," said DJ. "Let's put a photo of the dress too. It's pretty identifiable."

"Give me five minutes," called Casey as she headed back to the computer station.

"Any of you girls want to come with us?" asked Lane hopefully.

"I probably need to stick around," DJ told him. "My grandmother isn't functioning too well just now."

"I can stay with her," offered Rhiannon.

"It might be helpful to have you along," Conner pointed out. "I mean, a bunch of guys out looking for a girl could be taken wrong."

"Let me check with Marsha," DJ told him.

Marsha was still in the living room with her laptop open and talking into her Bluetooth. "Yes, I got that, Carl. Two thousand eight, white Nissan, two-door." She wrote down a license number. "That's great. No hotel yet? Okay, he might've used another name. No, keep checking." She turned to DJ now. "Anything new?"

DJ told her about their idea to check out the spring break hot spots. "And Casey is making some posters with Eliza's photo and the dress she wore."

Marsha nodded. "And here's what Ted is probably driving." DJ copied down the car information.

"Make sure you all leave your cell phone numbers here," Marsha told her. "And stay in touch." She held up a warning finger. "And don't let anyone play hero. Just keep track of your whereabouts and call me or nine-one-one if you see them. But do not approach them, understand?"

"And is your grandmother able to answer the phone?" Marsha asked suddenly. "I heard she wasn't feeling well."

"Yes," Rhiannon called out from the other room. "I just checked on her and she's better now."

DJ returned to the kitchen where everyone was gathered and waiting. "Okay, you guys, before we do anything, I want everyone to bow their heads and pray. I don't care whether you're a believer or not. But no one goes on this search unless we pray first."

"I agree," said Taylor.

"And I'll begin," offered Conner as he bowed his head and started to pray. DJ prayed once he had finished, and then Taylor, Rhiannon, and Bradford. To DJ's surprise even Casey prayed briefly. Harry and Lane actually said a few words and finally Conner said, "Amen!"

Then they all wrote down cell phone numbers for Marsha and headed their separate ways. DJ asked Conner to drive the general's car, and Taylor and Harry came along. Casey and Seth went with Lane. Bradford stayed behind with Rhiannon.

"This really does feel like searching for a needle in a haystack," DJ admitted as she waited for Conner to tape another flyer outside of a popular hotel. It seemed young people were everywhere and half of the girls looked strikingly similar to Eliza.

"What is it with all these blondes?" Harry complained. "Don't girls know that there's more than one hair color to choose from?"

Taylor laughed. "And fortunately not *all* gentleman prefer blondes."

"Quiet," said DJ suddenly. "My phone's ringing." She saw the caller ID as she opened it. "It's Eliza's cell," she said quietly. "*Hello?*" No one spoke on the other end. "*Eliza?*" said DJ. "I saw your name. I know it's you. Speak to me!" Still nothing besides some scritch-scratch static sounds. "Eliza, if you can hear me, make some kind of noise. Or text message, Eliza. Text us!" But then she lost the connection.

"Call her back," commanded Conner.

"Maybe she doesn't want her phone to ring," DJ told him. "Maybe she's hiding or something."

"I'm going to call Marsha," said Taylor as she got out of the car.

Just then DJ's phone trilled.. "It's a text message," DJ said. "It says *Motel*."

They all waited impatiently for another text, but DJ's phone was silent.

"At least we know she's at a motel," Conner said.

"Yeah, there are only dozens around here," Taylor reminded him.

Just then DJ's phone rang again. "Another text," she told them. "It's just the number six."

"*Motel Six!*" yelled Harry as he leaped out of the car to tell Taylor.

Taylor relayed this to Marsha then hopped back into the car. "They're on it," she told them. "Apparently there aren't that many Motel Sixes in the Palm Beach area."

"If she's really in the Palm Beach area," said DJ.

"What do we do now?" asked Harry.

"Hey, I saw a Motel Six sign on the way home from the train station this morning," Conner told them. "I thought if Lane and I got into some kind of fight over DJ I might end up there."

DJ laughed. "Like that's going to happen."

"I know it's a long shot, but want to check it out?"

"Why not?" DJ nodded. "But remember what Marsha said—no heroics. If we see anything suspicious, we just call her."

"It's probably not the right hotel anyway," Harry said from the back.

"Eliza might not even be in the Palm Beach area," Taylor pointed out.

"Well, it beats sitting on our hands." DJ was looking out the window, keeping a watch out for a two-door white Nissan. Unfortunately, it was a fairly common-looking car.

"There's the motel sign," Conner called out.

"You should've turned back there," Harry told him. "That was the entrance."

"I'll just go on around," he said.

"Yeah, circle the building," teased DJ.

But as he was going around the back side, DJ spotted a car that actually fit the description. "Don't slow down or stop," she told him. "But everyone look at the white Nissan parked between the Black SUV and the red car and see if you can read the plate."

"That's it!" shouted Taylor. "That's the car."

"No way," said Harry. "Are you sure?"

Conner was slowing down now, craning to see the license plate.

"No," DJ told him. "Just drive on by and act natural in case someone is looking." She squinted, trying to read the numbers. But Harry was already spouting them out and they matched what DJ had on the paper in front of her.

"*Marsha*?" Taylor was already on the phone. "We found his car!" There was a quick pause. "Yes, the numbers are the same. No, Conner just drove right past and no one is around. I'm not sure of the address but it's not too far from the Amtrak station. Yes, that sounds right. Okay." Taylor closed her phone. "She's sending someone."

"Hey," said Harry. "I see a blonde girl in a black and pink dress."

DJ turned around to see.

"Don't let them see you looking!" Conner commanded.

"It's her!" DJ exclaimed. "And there are TWO guys!"

"I think one of them has a gun," Harry said quietly, "underneath the jacket that's draped over his arm."

"That's Ted—he's pushing Eliza into the backseat of the car," Taylor whispered. "The other guy is older and he's driving."

"Grab that parking space around the corner," DJ told Conner. "The rest of us stay down."

"Why?" asked Harry.

"Ted—he's seen Taylor and me before."

"I'll just sit here until they drive past," Conner said in a surprisingly calm voice. He was pretending to read a map as they all silently waited for what seemed like several minutes, but was probably just seconds. "Okay," he told them, "they're out of sight. DJ and Harry trade seats—hurry. You girls stay down in the back. We're going to tail them." And just like that, they switched seats and Conner was following about four cars behind the kidnappers. Meanwhile Taylor was on the phone, and according to Marsha the police were on their way. "Yes," Taylor said to Marsha. "We're a safe distance away and Conner is being very careful. We just don't want to let them—"

"Taking a left on the street ahead," Conner told them.

"Palmetto," Harry yelled out.

"Left on Palmetto," Taylor said into the phone.

"Take your time, Conner," Harry was telling him. "Don't want to look like you're in a hurry. Nice and easy."

DJ's heart was pounding and she wanted to yell at Conner to go faster and not to lose them, but she knew it was better to be quiet. So she just kept her head down low and prayed. She didn't know how much time had gone by, but it felt like hours.

"I see a state police car," said Harry. "Coming up from behind us at a fairly fast clip."

"Are his lights on?" asked DJ hopefully.

"No."

"And I just saw what could be an unmarked car turning onto the street ahead of us—a slate-gray sedan," Conner said quickly. "Let's hope anyway."

"Oh, man, will you look at that!" exclaimed Harry.

"We can't see a thing!" Taylor shouted back.

"What's going on?" cried DJ.

"They just ran a stoplight," Conner exclaimed. "Right as a city police car came to the intersection. The black and white's got his lights on and is pulling them over."

"Hopefully the city cop knows what he's getting into," said Taylor.

"But talk about great timing."

"Hey, Conner, you better pull over too," Harry warned. "That cop behind you just put his lights on."

"That's right!" DJ called out. "Don't get too close — there could be a shootout!"

"Wow," said Harry. "This is like a movie."

"With less action," said Conner.

"Here comes action now!"

Suddenly DJ and Taylor poked their heads high enough to see from the back seat. Various cars were surrounding the vehicle and suddenly they were coming from every direction, with guns out and commands being given, and just like that the cops had both the driver and Ted outside and flattened out on the ground.

"That's more than enough action for me," DJ said with wide eyes. "Look, that cop looks like he's going to arrest Eliza." He had her face forward against the car with her hands up like she was a suspect too.

"They're just being careful," Conner told her. "You know, in case she has Stockholm Syndrome."

"Huh?"

"When the victim feels sorry for the kidnapper and does something crazy," Taylor explained.

"That doesn't seem to be the situation," Harry said as they turned her around. "She looks like she's about to go to pieces."

"Should we go offer to help her?" asked DJ.

"It might not hurt," said Taylor. "Eliza looks pretty rattled. Why don't you just drive a little closer and we can explain who we are."

Conner had barely stopped the car before DJ burst out and ran toward Eliza. The policeman near her looked like he was about to go for his gun. "Hold it right there," he shouted when she was about ten feet away from him.

DJ stopped in her tracks and actually put her hands up. "I'm a friend of Eliza's!"

"*DJ!*" cried Eliza with tears running down her face.

"Is it okay to come over there?" DJ asked tentatively.

He nodded. "But walk slowly—no fast moves."

DJ slowly approached and Eliza literally fell into her arms sobbing. "It's going to be okay," DJ kept telling her over and over. "You're safe now."

Before long, they let Taylor and the others gather around her, and after a few minutes Eliza was able to calm down. But DJ could still feel her shaking.

"We need to take you in to make a statement," a man in a sports jacket told Eliza. He showed her his badge. "I'm Detective Snyder with the Florida State Police. The FBI have been in contact with us. Do you want one of your friends to come along with us for moral support?"

Eliza nodded, still clinging to DJ like they were long-lost sisters. "Yes! I want my friend DJ with me. *Please.*"

"You're okay with that?" he asked DJ.

DJ felt her own eyes getting damp now. "Of course," she told him. "I'm glad to come. My grandmother Katherine Carter is Eliza's guardian. She runs a boarding house back in Connecticut. And Eliza's parents are vacationing in Nepal. We were here for spring break . . . it was supposed to be fun."

He nodded somberly as he led them to the unmarked car. "Your friend was lucky today. This could have gone down a lot differently."

"It was more than luck," she told him. "A lot of people were praying for Eliza."

He actually smiled now. "Eliza has some good friends."

Eliza continued to cling to DJ as he drove them to a nearby hospital. "Thank you for coming," she told DJ again and again. "Thank you!"

It wasn't easy for DJ to listen as Eliza gave her statement in a private room at the hospital, starting at the beginning, explaining how they met on the plane and how "Todd" seemed like such a nice guy. "He said he was a Princeton student," Eliza said sadly. "And the way he talked seemed believable. I never thought twice about giving him my phone number."

"Maybe you will next time," the detective told her.

Eliza went on to tell about his phone call on Tuesday and how she probably told him a little too much about herself. "I was feeling kind of low that day." She shook her head. "Saying how I might've been better off having gone to Nepal with my parents. Then we got to talking about parents and where we lived ... and I know now that I said too much."

"So he knew your parents were wealthy."

She nodded sadly. "Oh, yeah—he knew."

She answered more questions, explaining how Todd/Ted hadn't been what she'd expected when they'd gone out for drinks. "I told him that I thought it was a mistake and that he should take me back," she said as she continued to wring her hands. "And that's when it started to get weird."

"Weird in what way?"

"He kept giving me funny excuses and he said he needed to go pick something up from a friend first. And then everything got fuzzy."

"Fuzzy how?"

"Like I'd had too much to drink, but I'd only had one drink."

"Do you think he put something in your drink?"

She nodded. "Oh, yeah, I'm sure he did."

"What happened after that?"

"The next thing I remember I woke up with duct tape over my mouth and my hands and feet were tied." She started to cry again and DJ reached for her hand, holding it tightly. "I've never been so terrified. It took me awhile to remember what happened or where I was. The best I could tell was it was some fleabag hotel room, but I had no idea where." She used a tissue to wipe her eyes. "It was like the worst nightmare imaginable."

"Were both men there the whole time?" the detective asked.

"I'm not sure. It seemed like they took turns watching me. And I could tell they were trying to put together a plan."

"To get ransom money?"

"Yes. They couldn't reach my parents because they're in Nepal. So I gave them the number of the general's beach house."

"Where Mrs. Carter is staying?"

Eliza nodded. "I didn't know who else to call for help. I mean, I knew she couldn't get them the money they wanted, but I didn't know who else to call."

"You did it right," DJ assured her.

"Everything was so confusing and blurry. I'm sure they put sleeping pills in my water bottle."

DJ handed Eliza a fresh tissue and then got one for herself as Eliza told the rest of the story, how she finally found a note pad with Motel Six on it and how she managed to get her cell phone open. "I was trying to call nine one one," she explained, "but I accidentally hit speed dial and when I hit nine, I realized it was DJ's number. I was so rattled I couldn't even think. But when DJ said to text her, it came together." She looked sadly at DJ. "Thanks."

He asked a few more questions and finally seemed satisfied. "Claire will take it from here," he told her.

"We have a doctor ready to give you a full exam and treatment," Claire told Eliza. "We'll collect evidence and then I think you will be allowed to go home."

"Don't leave me," Eliza pleaded with DJ.

"Don't worry," DJ told her. "I won't."

Finally they were done, and DJ had learned a whole lot more about crime and the legal system than she had ever wanted to know. But she kept reminding herself that she was doing this for a friend. And sure, it seemed a little ironic that it took something this horrific for Eliza Wilton to finally acknowledge DJ as her "friend." But maybe that was partly DJ's fault too. Maybe she should've tried harder with Eliza before things had spun so completely out of control.

"How's Eliza doing?" Taylor asked DJ after she came out from her last visit with her for the evening. Things had finally quieted down in the house. The guys had returned to their place, and the general had arrived and was visiting with Grandmother, who seemed to be recovering from her stress as well.

"Not bad considering." DJ sighed as she kicked off her flip-flops. "She actually said that she wants to go shopping on Saturday."

"No way!" Taylor just shook her head.

"Casey even volunteered to go with her. They're in there discussing it now."

"It's probably Eliza's only form of therapy."

"I told her she needs God more than she needs a new outfit."

"What did she say?"

"Just that God probably wouldn't mind if she got a new outfit too."

Taylor laughed. "He probably wouldn't."

DJ went into the bathroom to brush her teeth and Taylor followed. "Hey, maybe we should all go shopping with Eliza on Saturday. You know, as a show of our sisterhood and support."

DJ spit and then grimaced at the thought of an Eliza-style shopping trip. "That's more of a sacrifice for some of us than others."

"But you'll do it, won't you?"

DJ nodded and dropped her toothbrush into the glass.

"Did Casey tell you she broke up with Seth?"

"Seriously?" DJ was shocked, but pleased.

"Yep. I had that little talk that I'd been meaning to have with her. I think she saw the light. Or sort of."

"Well, as horrible as this whole ordeal with Eliza has been, I think it's a sobering reminder to all of us ... we need to make smarter choices."

Taylor nodded. "And it's weird because I've replayed some of the totally stupid things I've done the past couple of years. I mean, things that were way more dangerous than giving a guy my phone number. And I realize that I've been extremely lucky."

"And God was watching out for you."

"But not for Eliza?" Taylor fluffed her pillow.

"Hey, the way we found Eliza today was nothing short of a miracle. Even Marsha said as much."

"That's true."

DJ yawned and leaned back onto her bed. "I think I could sleep for about a week now."

"I'll sleep a lot better knowing that Tom Jones isn't about to kidnap one of us tonight."

"Thanks for reminding me." DJ sat up. "Did you lock the door?"

"Of course."

Eliza wanted to keep a low profile on Friday. Despite Grand-mother's varied attempts to reach Eliza's parents, they were still in the dark over what their daughter had just been through. Not that Eliza seemed to mind. In fact, at one point she begged Grandmother and the rest of them not to tell any-one about her ordeal. She just wanted to pretend that none of it had happened. Her escape was to hang in her room, watch TV, read fashion rags, eat real junk food, and visit with her "friends." Just the girls and not the guys, however.

Eliza made it clear that her room was off limits to any and all males. Even the general, not that he was anxious to see her. But it was funny because suddenly Eliza was acting like all of the Carter House girls were her very best friends. Like they really were sisters and that she would always hold each of them near and dear in her heart. DJ knew that this change in Eliza was the direct result of the kidnapping—a horribly high price to pay for friendship. But at least something good had come out of what was truly evil.

By Saturday afternoon, when the girls went on their big shopping spree, Eliza resorted back to some of her old ways—like playing the princess—but then she'd catch her-self and stop. Like she was actually trying. And she treated them all to lunch.

Finally, it was Sunday. The guys had already boarded the morning train to take them back to Connecticut, and the girls were getting ready to leave in a few hours too. DJ decide to hit the beach outside of the general's house, wanting to enjoy one last barefoot walk through the warm sand and maybe find a shell for a keepsake.

She was surprised to find that Casey was out there too.

"Hey, great minds think alike," DJ said as she sat next to Casey on the beach.

Casey jumped in surprise. "Oh, I didn't even hear you."

"Sorry, I didn't mean to startle —" Suddenly DJ realized that Casey was crying. "Are you okay?"

Casey sniffed and nodded. But then she started to cry even harder.

"Do you want to be alone?" DJ asked.

Casey just shrugged and looked out over the water.

"Do you want to talk?"

Casey's lower lip was quivering and DJ could tell something was really wrong.

"Is this about Seth?" DJ asked quietly. "I know you guys broke up and everything. Are you feeling sad about it?"

"Kinda, but not exactly."

"So ... do you miss him, Case? Like maybe you knew a side to him that we didn't, maybe he was actually really nice to —"

"That's not it." Casey turned and looked at DJ with frightened eyes. "I think I might be pregnant."

DJ didn't know what to say.

"I know what you must be thinking. That I'm stupid and irresponsible and a totally moronic idiot and why would I let —"

"No, of course, not, Casey. It's just that I'm ... well, I'm kind of in shock."

"Me too."

"Are you sure about this?" DJ asked hesitantly. "I mean, that you might be pregnant."

"If you're asking have I done a pregnancy test, the answer is no."

"Then how do you know ... I mean, what makes you think you really are?"

"You mean how did I get this way?" Casey looked sadly at DJ. "Even you have to know *that* answer."

"I know. That's not what I meant." DJ struggled to think. "I mean, have you missed a period?"

"No."

DJ brightened. "Okay, then you don't really know."

But Casey just shook her head.

"Okay, but you think you could be." DJ decided to back up. "What makes you think you could be? Other than the fact that you've obviously had sex?"

"Because things feel different — something inside of me has changed. I can just feel it."

"But maybe it's just because you're sad about breaking up. Or maybe, like me, you're emotionally wiped out from the crud we went through with the kidnapping and —"

"No, it's more than that."

DJ shook her head. "I just don't understand how you can be so sure you're pregnant, Casey. Not just because you *feel* different."

"Because I did some calculating," she said quietly. "And it was the wrong time of the month to have *unprotected* sex. Does that answer your question?"

"Unprotected?" DJ frowned. "Casey, why would you —"

"See, I knew you'd think I was the stupidest girl on the planet."

"No, I don't think that. I'm just surprised."

"If it makes you feel better, it wasn't my idea."

"Somehow that doesn't surprise me."

"Seth pushed me — and I gave in."

DJ just nodded.

"It didn't help that I'd been drinking."

She nodded again. She so didn't want to say something cold and harsh like "I told you so." Instead, she literally bit her tongue.

"How could I have been so dumb?" Casey sobbed as she threw her arms around DJ. "What am I going to do? My life is ruined! My parents will kill me!"

DJ hugged Casey. "Well, first of all, you're going to remember that you have good friends, Casey. Friends who really love you. And next you are going to hear a good friend telling you something very important."

Casey pulled back and looked at DJ. "What?"

"That you need God in your life. You really, really do, Casey. I'm sorry if it's not what you want to hear, but it's the truth. You need God's help more than ever right now."

"I know."

"You know?"

Casey nodded. "Not that it changes anything."

"It might not change the fact that you're pregnant—if you really are—but it will change what happens next in your life. I mean, if you let God in, if you ask him to help you, Casey, I know that he will. But I also know he won't force himself on you."

Casey nodded and slowly stood. "I probably shouldn't have told you that, DJ. I mean I could be wrong. Like you said, I haven't even done a test. Maybe I'm just imagining this whole thing. So don't take it too seriously, okay? And please don't tell anyone."

"I won't." DJ stood and looked Casey in the eyes. "But you better take what I told you seriously."

"Yeah … " Casey nodded and backed away. "I'll be thinking about it." And then she took off running toward the house.

DJ just sat there slowly shaking her head. *Why? Why? Why?* It seemed like some people had to be whacked around and beaten practically into a bloody pulp before they got the sense to ask God for help. *Why was that?* Was it that some people simply enjoyed pain? Or were they really that thick-headed? Or just plain hopeless? But why did some people have to hit rock bottom before they realized they needed to look up?

Yet even as she asked these frustrating questions, she knew that God already knew all the answers . . . and in the same way she knew that she could be part of some answers. Because, more than ever, she knew that God was using her and that he would continue to use her to reach into her friends' lives. And that was okay. In fact, it was better than okay. It was actually pretty cool.

last dance

melody carlson
bestselling author

Read this bonus chapter of *Last Dance*, Book 8 in the Carter House Girls series.

"I can't believe it's only six weeks until graduation." Kriti groaned then turned her attention back to the history book in her lap.

"If anyone doesn't need to worry about graduation, it's you, Kriti." Taylor reached for the fruit platter. "You've got it made it the shade, girl."

Kriti gave Taylor a half smile. But DJ knew Kriti wasn't concerned about graduating—that was a given. Kriti was obsessed with getting top honors at Crescent Cove High, even more so since she recently received her letter of acceptance from Harvard.

"Hopefully none of the Carter House girls need to worry about graduation." Grandmother scanned the girls around the breakfast table. "I can only assume that all of you are maintaining your grades."

"Of course," DJ assured her. Naturally, she wasn't going to admit what *kind* of grades that they were all maintaining. And DJ had actually been applying herself to her studies for most of the year. In fact, since returning to classes after spring break, it seemed that all the girls had gotten more diligent about school … and life in general. How long this sense of serious sobriety (both figuratively and literally) would last was anyone's guess. But DJ was not complaining.

"Here's a thought." Eliza's eyes lit up. "Instead of focusing on how long it is until graduation, why not focus on the fact we have only two weeks until prom."

"Like it's possible to forget," DJ tossed back at her. "Everywhere you turn in school there's a glossy, glitzy poster in your face—and half of them belong to Miss Eliza Wilton."

"So you've probably noticed the rest of them belong to Madison Dormont and Haley Callahan," retorted Eliza. "And I would really appreciate it if the Carter House girls would back me in my campaign a little more." She looked hopefully at Grandmother. "Don't you agree, Mrs. Carter? Shouldn't we all support each other like a family?"

Grandmother gave DJ a frustrated look. She'd already questioned why DJ had no interest in running for prom queen, but DJ had adamantly answered, "No way!" Grandmother now smiled and nodded. "Yes, of course, Eliza, all the girls should be perfectly willing to help you. It would be wonderful to have a Carter House girl as prom queen."

"Great. I'm going to have a campaign strategy meeting Sunday night and I'd like all of you to attend." Eliza beamed. "And it will be catered."

DJ suppressed the urge to say *whooptie do!*

"And I thought this weekend might be a good time for everyone to model their gowns," Eliza continued, this time aiming her words at Grandmother. "We can have a fashion critique night with Mrs. Carter as judge. Doesn't that sound like fun?"

Fun like a root canal, thought DJ.

"Not everyone's dress will be ready this weekend," Rhiannon protested.

Eliza nodded knowingly in DJ's direction. "Yes, so I've heard. Some girls seem to be dragging their heels—as if they think the Fairy Godmother is going to show up and wave her magic wand ... right, DJ?"

DJ laughed. "Yeah, that sounds like a good idea to me."

Eliza had been pestering everyone about prom dresses for the past couple of weeks now—ever since her mom had shipped her a beautiful gown from Paris, which she'd already sent out for alterations. So far only Kriti had caved to the pressure, allowing Eliza to drag her out formal shopping last weekend. Kriti probably gave in just to shut Eliza up so she could study without interruption.

"But what will you wear if the Fairy Godmother doesn't show?" continued Eliza. "Your soccer uniform perhaps?"

DJ rolled her eyes. "Give me a break, Eliza. I'll have a dress in time for the prom."

"I can only imagine what kind of lame dress you'll manage to dig up at the last minute. And, please, don't go to one of those rental places." Eliza made an expression that strangely resembled Grandmother. "Honestly, DJ, why do you insist on waiting until the last minute for anything that's remotely related to fashion? It's like you get some kind of thrill out of being difficult."

DJ just shrugged and picked up her coffee cup. She was tempted to remind Eliza that DJ wasn't the only one without a prom dress. But what difference would it make? Once

Eliza got stuck on something like this, she was like a pit bull. Sure, she might be a pit bull dressed in a pink Marc Jacobs jacket and lip gloss—but a pit bull all the same. Lately DJ had begun to suspect this fixation on prom was simply Eliza's cover-up ... a way to conceal the troubles that lay beneath. Even the fact that she and Lane had recently begun dating felt like a distraction device. It seemed that Eliza was so caught up in creating her "perfect" little world that she never had time to think about the traumatic kidnapping incident in Palm Beach a couple weeks ago. Like it had never even happened. And, according to Rhiannon (Eliza's roommate), Eliza had lied to Grandmother, saying that she'd informed her parents about the whole thing when she really hadn't.

"FYI," Taylor announced lightly, "DJ and I will be going prom dress shopping this weekend." She glanced at DJ. "Right, Roomie?"

DJ shrugged then noticed that Grandmother was eyeing her with interest. "That sounds like a good plan, DJ. Just don't forget we have modeling class on Saturday morning. You girls all know that the Mother's Day Fashion Show is only three weeks away, but you might not know it's completely sold out. It could well be Crescent Cove's biggest fundraising event ever. Just this week, Mayor Daschall told me how proud he is of the Carter House girls. He wants the newspaper to do a feature article on you girls the week before the fashion show. He's actually calling you girls the future first citizens of the next generation."

DJ held back the groan that was threatening to erupt as her grandmother droned on about how the Carter House girls were such fine examples. Was the mayor as delusional as Grandmother? Or were they all in deep, deep denial? Even so, DJ felt a tiny stab of pity for the old woman. She actually seemed to care about the girls … and she'd been a pretty good sport these past few weeks—especially in light of what they'd all gone through during spring break. DJ had honestly expected Grandmother to send all the girls packing once they'd gotten home. But, other than a rather lengthy lecture and stern warning about abiding by the house rules, she hadn't. As a result DJ had been trying to be more positive and cooperative lately. But hearing the mayor's praise of the girls made DJ want to scream. If only he knew the truth.

As Grandmother wound down her little pep talk, Casey quietly excused herself. It seemed that everyone at the table was subdued now. Perhaps they all felt a bit of guilt. *Future first citizens of the next generation* … with the kinds of problems these girls had experienced this past year? It was psychotic.

And, unless DJ was mistaken, their problems weren't over with yet. DJ watched as Casey silently exited the dining room. It felt like Casey was trying to slip beneath the radar, like she had something to hide. DJ honestly didn't know what to make of her anymore. Despite the fact that Casey had retracted the confession she'd made at Palm Beach, DJ still had a feeling that it could be true.

Oh, she knew it made no sense, but she still had this nagging fear that Casey really could be pregnant. And yet Casey had firmly denied this possibility. She'd explicitly told DJ that she'd been mistaken—*false alarm, no harm no foul, end of story*. And after that she refused even to discuss it. And, really, why would Casey lie? DJ just needed to let it go and forget about it.

Of course, it didn't help matters that Casey had started dating Seth again. Oh, like the other Carter House girls, she'd definitely calmed down her social life these past few weeks, but DJ had been disappointed to see Casey and Seth still together. Didn't Casey get that Seth was bad news? Didn't she see the way he treated her, how he took her for granted, and how he was after only one thing? Still, just like Taylor had hinted more than once, maybe DJ needed to back off. "All you can do is warn her and wait," Taylor had said. "You start pushing her and she'll probably just go the other direction." And Taylor should know since she'd been there herself not so very long ago.

Just the same, DJ found it hard to give up on her old friend and that's why she excused herself and hurried off in hopes of catching Casey. She'd invite her to shop for prom dresses. But Casey had already grabbed her bag and was on her way back down.

"Hey, Case," DJ said as she casually blocked the way. "Why don't you come shopping with Taylor and me on Saturday?"

Casey's brow creased. "Well, for one thing, I'm just about flat broke."

"But I thought you were going to the prom with Seth— don't you need a dress?"

"I do. But Rhiannon offered to help me with it."

"Oh … that's nice of her."

"Maybe … " Casey's scowl deepened. "In exchange I have to go to youth group with her for the next three weeks."

DJ grinned. Score points for Rhiannon!

"Yeah, it figures that would make you happy."

DJ heard the other girls coming out of the dining room. They'd be heading for the stairs and their last-minute grabs before school.

"It's just that I care about you," DJ said quickly. "And I'd really like to talk to you—"

"Later." Casey cut her off, pushed past her, and hurried down the stairs.

Carter House Girls Series from Melody Carlson

Mix six teenage girls and one '60s fashion icon (retired, of course) in an old Victorian-era boarding home. Add boys and dating, a little high school angst, and throw in a Kate Spade bag or two ... and you've got the Carter House Girls, Melody Carlson's new chick lit series for young adults!

Mixed Bags
Book One

Stealing Bradford
Book Two

Homecoming Queen
Book Three

Viva Vermont!
Book Four

Lost in Las Vegas
Book Five

New York Debut
Book Six

Spring Breakdown
Book Seven

Last Dance
Book Eight

Available in stores and online!

ZONDERVAN
.com